His

She lay upon the altar. Her face was alabaster, and her hair was gold, flowing behind her, beneath her, ... lay as ... at a wake.

Her eyes were closed, and she lay in beauty, as if she were sleeping.

But she wasn't asleep.

A red ribbon seemed to adorn her neck, but it wasn't a fashion accessory.

And it wasn't a ribbon.

It was a line of blood. Blood that streamed from her throat to the floor.

He screamed, but his scream was silent, no matter how hard he tried to make it into sound. He fought the mist and shadow mire that held him down as he tried to run to her, but he couldn't reach her…

"Mark!" The sound of his name was like an off button for the scene unfolding in his mind.

KEEPER OF
THE DAWN

HEATHER GRAHAM

MILLS & BOON

First published in Great Britain 2013
by Mills & Boon, an imprint of Harlequin (UK) Limited,
Eton House, 18-24 Paradise Road, Richmond, Surrey TW9 1SR

© Slush Pile Productions, LLC 2013

ISBN: 978 0 263 90412 3
ebook ISBN: 978 1 472 00676 9

089-0913

Harlequin (UK) policy is to use papers that are natural, renewable and recyclable products and made from wood grown in sustainable forests. The logging and manufacturing processes conform to the legal environmental regulations of the country of origin.

Printed and bound in Spain
by Blackprint CPI, Barcelona

New York Times bestselling author **Heather Graham** has written more than a hundred novels, many of which have been featured by the Doubleday Book Club and the Literary Guild. An avid scuba diver, ballroom dancer and a mother of five, she still enjoys her south Florida home, but loves to travel as well, from locations such as Cairo, Egypt, to her own backyard, the Florida Keys. Reading, however, is the pastime she still loves best, and she is a member of many writing groups. She's currently vice president of the Horror Writers' Association, and she's also an active member of International Thriller Writers. She is very proud to be a Killerette in the Killer Thriller Band, along with many fellow novelists she greatly admires. For more information, check out her website, theoriginalheathergraham.com.

Prologue

Illusion and Truth

Mark Valiente slowly became aware of himself, as if he were emerging from a trance where he had forgotten all movement and sense of place. He heard music, the volume slowly rising in his head. It was beautiful music—harps and violins, guitars and an organ playing while a drum kept the beat. He recognized songs, popular and classical, being performed as if for an audience.

Mist seemed to clear around him, and he realized he was in a church. It was beautiful, old, designed in the Gothic style, with elegant stained-glass windows. As he walked in, he saw that it was crowded with people. The men were dressed in suits, and the women were beautiful in dresses of what he thought of as spring colors, white and pastels, as well as hats and heels. Their heads turned, and they all smiled and looked benignly at him.

He walked down the aisle. Dead ahead, he saw that Brodie McKay was there, near the altar, grinning sheepishly and watching him as if Mark were about to do something that would change the world. The place, the people, the music, the very vibe…everything was absolutely beautiful, filled with light and promise. Colors seemed to spill through the stained-glass windows and paint the church, the red velvet runner, and everything and everyone around him, in a flow of bright and gentle tones. He glanced to his side, and he didn't see the people in the pews. Instead he saw a rather pale reflection of himself in one of the windows—which, of course, with the light streaming through, wasn't really possible. But there he was. Dressed in a charcoal-gray, somewhat-old-fashioned tux, red vest with a white shirt beneath. His tawny hair was neatly clipped and his face shaved. He almost smiled, thankful that he had cleaned up well for the event.

The event…

It was a wedding. *His* wedding. He would walk through the church and greet the crowd, and take his place next to Brodie, who was certainly his best man.

And then *she* would walk down the aisle.

Yes, he was waiting for her. He felt as if he were trembling; he had fallen in love. She was beautiful, and he dreamed of lying beside her naked, feeling the softness of her skin and the desire she awakened in him. And the way he felt when they'd made love and when he awoke to see her eyes. He was going to marry her...and she was the dream that had filled his soul. This moment, this marriage, would be consummate magic, an affirmation of all that lay between them.

He knew that he loved her.

He just...

...didn't know her name. Didn't even know who she was.

Somewhere in the back of his mind he mocked himself for the daydream.

He wasn't even dating anyone in particular.

And yet...

He could feel this; it wasn't just a vision in his mind's eye. It seemed to be something that was real to all his senses and in his soul.

Somehow he knew that they had chosen music from Zeffirelli's 1968 version of *Romeo and Juliet* for that moment when she would walk down the aisle.

But even as he moved forward, the light from the windows began to change. What had been bright now turned to dark, swirling purple and shades of gray. What had seemed like a glow of happiness and expectation filling the church became fear and dread. He saw the people around him, saw the smiles fade and the horror creep onto their faces....

And then those people evaporated. Brodie was gone. The music was strident and off-key, quieting to silence as the shadow colors merged to near-total darkness, leaving odd shapes and illusions to creep and crawl in the midst of a gray miasma.

He was still in the church. The only color that remained was the red runner beneath his feet. Before him, he saw something on the altar. Something in a shimmering mist of crystals and pearls and white.

His bride.

He felt his limbs grow heavy with fear and denial. He tried to run, but the fog was like sludge, and he couldn't reach her quickly enough. She was lying upon the altar, her face alabaster and her hair gold, flowing beneath her head and shoulders and falling in curls as if on a white pedestal at a wake.

Her eyes were closed and she lay in beauty, as if sleeping.

But she wasn't sleeping.

A red ribbon seemed to adorn her neck, but it wasn't an accessory.

And it wasn't a ribbon.

It was a line of blood that streamed from her throat to the floor, and then ran and created the very runner beneath his feet.

He screamed, but his scream was silent, no matter how hard he tried to make it into sound. He fought the mist and shadow mire that held him back, and he tried to run to her, but he kept slipping in the blood. *Her* blood. And the shadow creatures seemed to be holding on to him, throwing their heavy weight against him, keeping him from moving forward. She was dead, or dying, and he couldn't reach her....

"Mark!" The hushed sound of his name was like an off button for the scene unfolding in his mind.

He started as someone poked his arm.

He blinked. It had been so real, that…well, *vision* was the only word he could think of.

"Let's go." That was Brodie speaking.

Time, Mark knew, was a deceptive concept. That vision had seemed to go on forever, but, he realized now, only split seconds had passed in which he had either dozed off or been daydreaming. He wasn't in a church; he was in an unmarked police car parked off the road cutting through Starry Night Cemetery, and he and Brodie had been in the car, drinking coffee to stay alert—there was irony for you—since four in the afternoon.

Now his partner had seen something, something *he* should have seen, as well.

Brodie was already out of the car. Mark quickly followed suit.

Brodie headed for the Hildegard vault. Built by Sebastian Hildegard in 1920, it now housed several dozen bodies. Bodies belonging to a long line of lords and ladies of illusion and their various offspring.

Shapeshifters. Hell, yeah, they made great magicians.

Brodie motioned to him, and Mark nodded; they'd worked together often enough over the years to develop a silent shorthand. Brodie would take the front, while Mark slipped in by the rear door. Brodie had the power of his strength, while they both knew that Mark had a different means of entry. He'd perfected the powers of his kind years ago and was almost as adept at illusion as the Hildegard family.

They parted ways. Starry Night had been a private cemetery for the first seventy-five years of its existence, until Able Hildegard had taken over the family's holdings at his father's demise. The cemetery had been sold, and the then-living had scrambled to buy up plots and vaults so they might rest eternally with the famous who had found their way into the glorious grounds where illusionists and stars of stage and screen—silent and otherwise—had come for the peace of the ages. The truly dead *did* lie here, while others merely…rested. But, most of the time, it was a place of peace.

Or had been.

Until the living had begun to go missing and then turn up dead—and the trail of clues had led them here.

As Mark neared the iron-gated rear entry to the grand mausoleum, he could hear chanting. He edged closer, at first just listening and letting his eyes adjust so he could see what was happening inside the imposing vault. Night had fallen, but there was light within, spawned from torches that burned in the hands of those who stood around the sarcophagus of Sebastian Hildegard.

The marble lid of the sarcophagus was sculpted to resemble the grand patriarch of the family; in effigy

Sebastian lay with his hands folded over his chest, the long flowing robe of a magician almost real due to the energy of the artist's creation. But as Mark watched, a caped figure, with a golden face mask, stepped forward carrying a burden—a woman. She was blonde, and she wore a white halter dress. With her hair falling around her, it was impossible to tell whether she was unconscious…or dead.

Her fingers twitched. So, she wasn't dead, Mark thought.

Yet.

No sign of Brodie, but the chanting in the tomb was growing louder. Friends in the Otherworld of the Los Angeles area had warned them that they'd been hearing tales about the old Hildegard tomb. There was a cult growing up around the famous magician, a belief that blood sacrifices made on the altar of his sarcophagus would bring him back to life, and bring stardom, power and glory to those who worshipped at his feet.

Bull!

A dead shapeshifter was a dead shapeshifter.

But that didn't mean there weren't those out there who were willing to believe.

The woman was draped over the marble effigy of Sebastian Hildegard.

He feared they were out of time.

The gate was locked. No matter. It was old and easy to force. The iron hinges must have been kept well-oiled, because they didn't even squeak until he was in, and once there, he was ready.

"LAPD! Stop where you are!" he ordered.

Someone let out a shriek of fury. A flutter of cloth and shadow erupted in the room; the woman was left behind as figures began to scramble and torches fell.

"There are silver bullets in this gun," Mark warned. "Stop!"

That wouldn't mean a lot to a number of those here, but to some—the Others in the group—it would be fair warning.

Something flew at him. It was a caped skeletal figure with a monstrous face, screaming as it moved. He raised his customized gun, aimed and fired just as it reached him. The thing disappeared, and his bullet crashed into the concrete slab of a tomb in the wall.

One figure tried to race past him, a human. He went down in a whining sprawl as Mark casually punched him, and then Mark cuffed him quickly before tackling another. The place was in chaos. Mist filled the room, and a horde of hooded figures and insubstantial shadows came at Mark, screeching incoherently. In the background, he could hear humans screaming and crying, followed by the sounds of Brodie intercepting those who tried to escape by the main entrance.

The fog began to clear. He met up with Brodie, and they looked around. Five humans—three men and two women—lay cuffed on the ground. The Others had gone, vanished, disappeared into thin air.

Or the mists of illusion.

"Maybe one of them will talk—tell us something we can use," Brodie said. Even he was breathing hard.

"Maybe," Mark agreed. But they both knew they had failed. Whoever was at the head of this mess wasn't one of the human beings lying cuffed on the floor and waiting to be taken to the station.

But the head of this particular operation was a shapeshifter. And they had missed him.

Or her.

"The woman… She can't be dead…. They needed her alive," Mark said, stepping over a cuffed man to reach the tomb of Sebastian Hildegard.

He lifted her carefully. Blond hair fell around her shoulders, revealing her face.

He nearly froze.

He'd already seen her tonight.

He'd never seen her in the flesh before, but…

She had been the woman in his daydream, the bride at his blood wedding….

"Alive?" Brodie asked him anxiously.

Her eyes opened, and she stared at Mark. They were sea-green and beautiful, and she looked disoriented.

Then she screamed and began to fight him, and she was damned good at it, belting him in the jaw and raking her nails across his face in fury. She stood on her own now; she seemed to have the strength of a thousand demons.

"Hey!"

Brodie came to his aid, catching her arms. "We're the cops! We're here to save you."

As Brodie spoke, they heard sirens in the night; his call for the bus, to haul those they had caught to lockup, was being answered.

The young woman blinked. She inhaled, staring at Mark. He realized suddenly that she wasn't human; she was Other. She was Elven.

Brodie whispered, "My God— Elven," just as Mark thought it. But then, to Mark's amazement, Brodie added a name. "Alessande Salisbrooke!"

Maybe it was natural that Brodie knew her; he was Elven, too.

She spun and looked at Brodie, and let out a sigh of relief. "Brodie. I didn't realize—"

She stopped midsentence and stared at Mark, heat and anger emanating from her. "Vampire," she said. "And you're a cop?"

"Yeah, I'm a cop," he said. She studied him as if he'd done something wrong, or as if his being a vampire was anathema to her. He felt his temper rising. "Yes, I am a vampire," he said angrily. "I'm the vampire who just saved your ass." He was shaken. He didn't usually strike out because a panicked victim fought him.

But...

He'd seen her in his vision. Seen her with a ribbon of blood coming from her throat...

At a wedding.

Their wedding.

That was certainly never going to happen.

"Saved me?" she exclaimed. "Vampire idiot. You ruined *everything*."

Chapter 1

"Seriously," Sailor Gryffald said, "what were you thinking, Alessande?" Sailor continued to pace while Alessande sat.

After a stop at the police station, Brodie and Mark had dropped Alessande off with Sailor and had gone straight to Pandora's Box, since Brodie had been anxious to see Rhiannon, the canyon's vampire Keeper—and his fiancée. Alessande was glad to be alone with Sailor and free to talk.

Sailor continued, "Those monsters were about to sacrifice you. Believe me, you helped save my life, so I know how competent you are, but no one knows what kind of evil you were really up against, if I understand what you're saying correctly."

Alessande winced. She really shouldn't have been

so angry with that vampire cop—after all, he *had* been trying to save her. But, in her own opinion, she had been prepared. Ready. And she was suspicious of vampires and...

No, she shouldn't have snapped at him.

"I had to be taken captive," Alessande explained wearily. "It was the only way for me to get in there and find out what's going on, who's behind the cult and the deaths." There was more to her logic—and her desperation to get at the truth—but at this moment she wasn't ready to completely explain herself, not even to Sailor Ann Gryffald.

"But...you're Elven," Sailor said sternly. In the world of the Others, Sailor was the Keeper of the Elven community in the L.A. Valley. "You're an *ancient!*"

No one liked to be reminded of her age, Alessande thought, arching a brow at Sailor.

"Sorry," Sailor said. She and her two Gryffald cousins—Rhiannon and Barrie—were new to the Keeper job, but all three had already been tested under fire. Alessande knew that because she'd been involved with helping Sailor find her way.

They'd met when Alessande had carried Sailor into her home after Sailor had been attacked during the recent so-called Celebrity Virus plague.

"Seriously," Sailor went on. I can't tell you how proud I am of so many in the Elven community, but we're not considered the...the toughest of the Others.

Alessande, you create potions, you're a healer. You live alone.... You're practically a hermit."

"Gee, thanks," Alessande said.

"I'm not trying to offend you, and you know it. You brew the best tea in the country—maybe in the world. You're like a beacon of caring and wisdom. But you're gentle. And you could have been up against were-creatures, vampires and God knows what else—not to mention very vicious human beings. How did you intend to save yourself in that situation?" Sailor demanded.

"I was going to teleport," Alessande said, indignantly.

"You can't teleport when you're unconscious," Sailor argued.

Alessande shook her head, desperately wanting to deny the seriousness of the situation, but the truth was she knew she might have gotten herself into trouble—serious trouble—and she should be grateful to the cops who had come to her rescue. She had just gotten it into her head lately that she had to be more proactive in protecting all Others—along with the human race. And that, of course, was because of Regina, because she'd been forced to see firsthand once again what could happen to the young and innocent—especially the young and innocent among the Elven.

Like the rest of the world, L.A. was filled with all manner of creatures most of humanity knew about only because of legend—and movies. Creatures that most humans didn't even believe in. Keepers—like the Gryffald cousins—were human beings, but... more. They had special powers aligned with those of the particular paranormal race they were tasked with protecting, and were generally born into long-time Keeper families. They bore special identifying birthmarks. It was as if their role had been predetermined by a divine power.

There were areas in the world where the Other races seldom desired to live...too hard to blend in, not enough for them to do.

L.A., however, was a haven for Others. Because it was a movie town, monsters and strange creatures abounded on-screen and, frankly, offscreen, given how many...unique individuals tended to migrate there. As a place to "hide in plain sight," nothing filled the bill like Hollywood. That meant that the area was densely populated by Others, so there had to be a commensurately large number of Keepers.

Elven, like Alessande, were fairly recent arrivals in the New World; they were creatures of the earth. Ocean voyages—that much time away from trees, from the rich soil—would have killed them. Alessande had only left the Old World herself when transatlantic flight started to become commonplace.

She was an ancient, one hundred six years old, though she knew she appeared—in the human world—to be about thirty. She'd seen a great deal of the wickedness the world had to offer—wickedness dealt out by both human beings and Others.

Despite everything she'd encountered, everything she had lived through, she had chosen to heal, to advise.

But, damn it, she was an ancient! She should have been able to overcome whatever drug had been given to her.

She'd been aware of everything as it had been going on, and to some degree she had been able to fight the drug, though she had feigned complete passivity.

But…they had drugged her, and it had definitely affected her. Would she have been able to escape at the last second?

Now she was at the Gryffald family estate, a small collection of historic homes on a nice little hill in Laurel Canyon, collectively named the House of the Rising Sun. Sailor's home was the main residence, and it was called Castle House, while on either side were the guesthouses: Gwydion's Cave, where Barrie lived, and Pandora's Box, where Rhiannon made her home. When their fathers, Keepers all, had been called away on international business, the cousins— Sailor, Rhiannon and Barrie—had been thrown into a game that was ages old, though mostly new to them, since they hadn't expected to take their places as Keepers for years to come, yet the land had been deemed for Keepers for decades. The property had originally belonged to a magician billed as "Merlin," real name Ivan Schwartz, who had been helped by the Gryffald cousins' grandfather. Schwartz had added the guesthouses to his estate so that the Keepers could live on his property if they chose. Before he died, Ivan had sold the estate to the Gryffald family for such a pittance that for all intents and purposes it had actually been a gift.

Of course, it came with a catch. Merlin was still around, haunting whichever house he chose. He was a very polite ghost, often extremely helpful, and totally respectful of the inhabitants' privacy, so in actuality he was a perfect tenant.

At the moment, though, Alessande was glad he wasn't haunting Castle House.

Keepers had watched over various communities of Others at least since the ancient days, before accepted magic had ended and the world had become a place where the unusual was feared and anyone different, even if they were human, was considered an enemy to be burned at the stake or otherwise destroyed. Because the cousins' fathers had been considered some of the wisest and most effective Keepers in the world, they had been called up to help form a council so that Others around the world would have guidance—and laws—to help them all live productive lives without attracting the kind of notice that would lead to a return of the bad old days.

Every Other—from the gnomes and leprechauns to the were-folk, vampires and shapeshifters—lived by the Code of Silence, keeping the very existence of the Otherworld secret from humanity. The Code was broken only occasionally and for very special human beings. Even the rashest Others, those with little respect for laws of any kind, upheld the Code, because the Code meant survival. Without it, they could all be doomed. While many in the Other community had powers that made them far stronger and far more lethal than human beings, the human population of the world was larger by perhaps 99 percent, and therefore the Others were vulnerable to persecution and death should their existence ever come to light.

Jonquil, Sailor's big ragamuffin of a mutt, whined softly and licked Alessande's fingers. She smiled and scratched the dog's head. If only the world were made up of such creatures as this. Jonquil seemed to instinctively know kind people from the cruel ones.

Sailor was doing very well as an Elven Keeper now, though when Alessande had first known her, she hadn't taken her position seriously at all. But that current knowledge gave Alessande a measure of confidence when she was speaking with her Keeper.

"I was always aware of what was going on," she said. "I know that I appeared to be unconscious, but there was a part of me that was *there*. I believe I could have teleported when the right moment came." Elven were strong, even if not as strong as vampires, and while they couldn't give the illusion of being someone—or some*thing*—different, as shapeshifters could, they were able to teleport, moving through space, very handy in escaping dangerous situations. No one yet knew the science of it, but being an Other often meant that there just weren't logical answers. No one really understood how shapeshifters managed to appear to be birds—and then fly away.

"*Believe* isn't good enough when your life depends on it," Sailor said sternly. She looked at Alessande. "Don't get me wrong. I know I wouldn't be where I am today, knowing what I know and doing my job with my mind focused on my responsibilities, if not for you. But, Alessande, I have to agree with Brodie and his vampire partner—you were risking your life, and you almost lost it."

Alessande smiled; she loved Sailor, and knew her Keeper was being completely sincere. Alessande had been both healer and coavenger when Sailor had fallen ill to the Celebrity Virus, then had brought justice to its perpetrator—since the plague's spread had been intentional. Alessande knew what she was doing when it came to dealing with the world's—and the Otherworld's—evils.

So she really didn't understand why Brodie was so upset with her. Brodie knew her, knew she was capable of handling herself when the going got tough. As for the vampire cop—well, he was a vampire, and she didn't expect a hell of a lot out of any vampire.

"Honestly, I knew what I was doing," Alessande insisted.

Jonquil barked as if in agreement.

"This is the kind of situation the police need to handle," Sailor said.

"The police? Oh, Sailor, come on. We both know

that, in situations where Others are involved, the police are all but helpless."

"That's why Others are encouraged to join law enforcement," Sailor said. "Whether you want to believe it or not, Brodie and Mark were anything but helpless at the cemetery."

"I don't care," Alessande said. "We have to be involved when it comes to our world, Sailor. You know that. And even if they did manage to arrest a number of cult members, we still don't know who's behind it all. Someone is at work out there doing something far more vicious than merely creating a cult, and they have to be an Other. I believe it's either a shapeshifter or a vampire, which is why it's not such a great thing for a vampire to be working on this. I mean, seriously, a vampire policeman is really something of an oxymoron!"

"Oh, Alessande, honestly, that isn't true," Sailor said. Her eyes were wide as she stared past Alessande, who swung around quickly in her seat to find Rhiannon Gryffald had arrived, standing with her hands on her hips, watching Alessande.

She winced.

No, of course it wasn't true, and she knew it. She didn't understand her own behavior right now—she was usually cool, collected and serene.

It was the situation.

And maybe even the fact that she had almost died, but she had to remain in denial or give up on her ultimate goal.

And now, just as she had spoken carelessly, Rhiannon had walked in.

Rhiannon Gryffald was the oldest of the three cousins, and though she had not particularly wanted to come to L.A. when her father had headed off to form the international council, she had been the first to embrace her life as a Keeper—the vampire Keeper for the Valley. And she was very much in love with Brodie.

Thankfully, Brodie was an Other—Alessande's kind, Elven—so there was no awkwardness in trying to explain the Otherworld and Rhiannon's role in it to him. He was a great guy and a good cop, and Alessande was fond of him—just as she was fond of the entire Gryffald family. But Rhiannon was quick, maybe too quick, to defend the basic decency of the Valley's vampire population—and quick to take offense if they were accused of misdeeds with no proof.

"I'm sorry," Alessande murmured.

"Vampires get a bad rap," Rhiannon said. She tossed back a length of auburn hair. "I knocked," she told her cousin. "I guess you didn't hear me— over the rant."

"Rhiannon," Alessande said, "really, I'm sorry. It's just that Brodie's partner behaved as if I was some kind of idiot with no idea what I was doing."

Rhiannon arched a brow. "You were about to be a sacrifice—if I heard correctly."

"I would have teleported at the right time," Alessande insisted stubbornly. "But first I would have figured out who's behind the cult and the killings. Never mind. I'm not trying to be argumentative or cast aspersions on anyone. But this is ridiculous. When we left the police station, I agreed to come here to talk with Sailor, as my Keeper, but if no one's going to take me seriously, then forgive me, but I really should be leaving."

She'd come straight here—from seemingly endless hours of police paperwork. From questions that she answered as best she could when there was no true answer to some of them, or no answer she could give in the world of men. She'd been very careful, trying to be forthright without giving away any information that would make the human employees of the police department suspicious.

And worse, her car was at the impound lot. She'd had to ride with Brodie and Mark, and she was stuck here until she could ease her way out of the conversation and get someone to drive her home.

She spoke in an even tone to Rhiannon. "Forgive me. This— It's senseless," she said quietly. "The fact that you're Keepers makes you responsible for dangerous situations, but it doesn't preclude the rest of us from acting when those we care about are threatened. I really would like to just go home now, if you don't mind."

"Alessande," Sailor protested gently. "We're not attacking you—really."

"No, I don't mean to attack," Rhiannon said softly.

"If it seems like we are, it's because we're frightened—frightened for you."

At that moment Barrie Gryffald, Keeper of the Valley shapeshifters, burst into the house. "I heard what happened! Oh, my God! Alessande—you're all right?"

"I'm fine, Barrie, thank you," Alessande said.

"But you set yourself up—were you able to find out anything about Regina?"

"Regina?" Rhiannon asked.

Alessande lowered her head for a moment. She looked up at Barrie and shook her head slowly. "No. I'd hoped I'd be taken wherever she might be and that…"

"And that you could save her," Barrie finished.

"She's innocent and young and…she disappeared two nights ago now. I'm afraid. The longer she's missing…"

Regina Johnson was eighteen and on her own. She'd come to L.A. straight out of a foster home in San Francisco. Alessande had met her when Regina had agreed to play a minor role in a fantasy movie being filmed at a small studio run by one of Alessande's friends. That was a negative about being Elven, at least in Alessande's mind. Many in the Elven community flocked to L.A. because they had excellent prospects for success in the movies. Elven tended to be blond, blue-eyed, statuesque and filled with a natural charm that the camera seemed to love. Elven who didn't work *in* the movies tended to work *on* them.

"All right, yes, I did—do—want to save her. But that's simply part of it. Okay, most of it," Alessande said in a rush. "But it's not only Regina. She was just the last to disappear, so there's still hope for her. And I feel so bad for her. Growing up, she didn't even know that she was Elven, didn't know that there was a whole community of Others just like her, that she was normal…and she comes here, settles in, starts to work—and disappears."

"You felt bad for an orphan because *you* were orphaned, weren't you?" Sailor said.

"Yes," Alessande admitted. Her situation hadn't been quite as bad. She had never known her own father, but she had a brother two years younger from her mother's second marriage; his father and their mother had been with them until dying in an accident when Alessande was seven and Conner five. After that they had been adopted by Elven parents and had grown up in a family where they were loved and understood. That had been back in Northern Scotland, many years ago. Her brother was still dear to her, but he'd remained behind in the Old World when she'd left in the middle of World War II, unable to stay behind after the love of her life had been killed during the invasion of Normandy. She loved her brother dearly, and one of them traveled back and forth every few years to visit. Her adoptive parents were still overseas as well, having chosen to retire to Cork, in Ireland. She saw them as often as she could.

Regina had not had the benefit of a brother or loving adoptive parents. She'd thought there was something seriously wrong with her for most of her life. Alessande had met her soon after she'd discovered what she was and had wanted to make the world right for her.

Then…

Then she'd been kidnapped—right when being kidnapped seemed to mean showing up dead just a few weeks later.

"The point is," Alessande said, "Regina was the third young woman to disappear—and the other two were apparently held somewhere for weeks before they were dumped."

"We all understand trying to save a friend," Barrie said. She walked over to the sofa in front of the fire and took a seat, looking around Castle House as if she were assessing it—as if she'd never been in it before. Like the guest cottages, Castle House was eclectic, filled with old charm and curios.

The houses seemed to suit the unique personalities of the three women. Castle House boasted carved-wood details, and Alessande loved it. Her own cabin was built of wood, which was always comforting to her, and from it, she drew her strength.

Barrie was apparently trying to figure out where to start. A reporter, she was up on the news almost as it happened. "It's true," she said now, looking over at Rhiannon. "Leesa Adair disappeared six weeks ago. Her body was found two weeks later and—" she paused, wincing "—and the medical examiner said that she'd only been dead a day or two. Judith Belgrave disappeared four weeks ago, and her body was found just two days ago. Whoever is kidnapping these women is holding them for weeks before they wind up dead."

Rhiannon had taken a seat on one of the overstuffed armchairs by the sofa, and now she looked from Alessande to Barrie. "But though they bled out, they were not truly drained. If a vampire were behind this, I guarantee you—a rogue vampire wouldn't waste a murder. Those girls would have not had one drop in their bodies."

Alessande winced. "I hate to say this, but usually when something involves magic and illusion—like this Sebastian Hildegard cult—shapeshifters are involved."

"Naturally I've thought about that," Barrie said quietly.

"Let's back up a minute," Rhiannon said, turning to Alessande. "Exactly how did you almost become a sacrifice to Sebastian Hildegard? Brodie and Mark were out at the cemetery earlier because an anonymous tipster had called and said that they suspected a 'cult meeting with murderous intent' would occur there at midnight. But what made you think that the cult was connected to the dead women and Regina's disappearance?"

"And how on earth did you arrange to get yourself taken?" Sailor demanded.

"And why, if they were holding the other women before killing them, did they decide to sacrifice you so quickly?" Barrie asked.

Alessande looked from one cousin to another.

"I read the news stories about the other women who were kidnapped and traced their routes—and I knew where Regina had gone the day she disappeared," Alessande explained. "She had just gotten a job at the House of Illusion when—"

Sailor interrupted her with a tone of anger and impatience. "There's been trouble there before," she said. "But you know I work there, right?"

"Yes, I know that," Alessande said.

"Between waitressing and performing there, I would have known if the House of Illusion was the last place those women were seen," Sailor said.

"It wasn't the last place they were seen," Alessande continued. "But both dead women *and* Regina were there within two days of their disappearances. Nearby is an old studio—"

"I know it!" Sailor said, her voice growing anxious. "It was owned by the Hildegard family. It closed down thirty years ago and the land has been the center of a legal dispute between the city and the heirs for years now."

"I know," Alessande said.

"That studio is surrounded by a seven-foot wall," Rhiannon said.

"And it's right by a coffee shop and a gas station and a convenience store," Alessande pointed out. "Regina called me the afternoon she disappeared. She was going to stop to get gas on her way home from the House of Illusion. And both of the other women had bought gas the day they went missing, too. Their cars were found with the tanks full."

"How do you know that?" Sailor asked her.

"I went by the police impound," Alessande said.

"And they just told you that?" Rhiannon asked.

"You found an officer, flirted with him—and read his mind, didn't you?" Barrie said.

Alessande flushed; as long as the Elven could get a person to look them straight in the eyes, yes. Teleporting and mind reading were their talents. It had been an easy matter for Alessande to learn everything she had wanted to know from the officer who had been on duty at the impound. He had been human—and blithely unaware of the Others around him.

"I didn't do anything illegal," Alessande said.

"I'm just annoyed that I didn't think of it," Barrie said.

"Okay, so let's get this in order," Rhiannon said. "You investigated at the House of Illusion—"

"Not really. I just watched the news reports and read their coverage. Leesa's boyfriend said she'd gone there with friends, and Judith's mother mentioned in an interview that her daughter had been there, too. Regina called me from the parking lot to say she'd gotten the job and was going to stop for gas on her way home…so I went to the House of Illusion, and looked around, saw the gas station and figured it made sense that they'd all filled up there. And with the old studio right next door, it just seemed logical there was a connection."

"And it didn't occur to you to call the police?" Rhiannon asked.

Alessande smiled. "If I'd called the police, they would have made some big-deal search, and everyone would have disappeared before anything was discovered. Plus they would need a warrant—and I didn't."

"There are also laws for Others," Rhiannon said. "In fact, they're being formalized by the international council right now. And for all of us to live as we do—with the right to the pursuit of life, liberty and happiness—we have to abide by the laws that govern us, as well."

"I didn't break any laws. I had dinner at the House of Illusion, watched the show, and then I bought gas and looked curiously through the gates at the old Hildegard Studio," Alessande explained. "And…"

"And?" Rhiannon asked.

"There's an opening in the gate where one of the bars is rusted out. So I slipped through and started to walk around."

"And then?" Sailor asked.

"And then some jerk threw a bag over my head," Alessande said.

"If he was human, you could have escaped," Sailor told her.

"But I wasn't trying to escape," Alessande explained. "I wanted them to take me wherever they were holding Regina."

"But I presume they didn't," Rhiannon said.

"I don't know. Probably not. I think they decided to kill me right away because they caught me snooping. Anyway, there was something…something on or in the bag that knocked me out for a while. I don't know what it was—I should have recognized the scent," Alessande said. She was an expert in herbs and herbal remedies. "But—" she quickly defended herself "—I was awake and aware by the time we got to the cemetery. They wouldn't have been able to sacrifice me."

She was startled by a loud snort and quickly spun around in her chair to see that Mark and Brodie had slipped in unnoticed. She wondered how long they had been listening.

"You were pretty damned out of it when I got there," Mark said.

She was about to reply when Brodie strode over and took up a position behind Rhiannon. "Alessande, you didn't say all this at the station."

"Seriously, Brodie? How could I?" she demanded.

"You could have told us that you were taken from the old Hildegard Studio," he said.

"No! Don't you understand? *We* have to get in there," she said. "Not the police. Besides, what should I have said? That I got some of my information through Elven mind reading?"

"Your sarcasm won't change anything. What you did was dangerous," Brodie told her.

"Please," she said, her aggravation evident. "Life for us is dangerous—that's why we have Keepers, and why we depend so heavily on one another. And why Elven look after Elven."

"You're not a Keeper," Brodie said firmly. "And you're certainly not a cop. So you were way out of line, doing what you did."

"What you did, what you tried to do, was very courageous," Rhiannon said. "But you shouldn't have acted on your own. We're a pretty strong group here. You've got four Keepers, counting Sailor's fiancé, Declan—plus you've got Brodie and Barrie's fiancé, Mick, who is an investigative reporter and shapeshifter. This…mission will involve all of us. Alessande, you're brilliant, an ancient. You create powerful potions to heal us. You can look at the world and see the truth. You have to be careful. We can't risk you, don't you know that?" she asked gently.

"Rhiannon, I appreciate that," Alessande said. "But if you recall, I was out there taking chances during the Celebrity Virus—and I will be out there now. Please. What I did was find out more than the cops. And what I am right now is really, really tired," she said, rising. "Sailor, would you mind giving me a ride home?"

"My car is blocking yours," Mark Valiente said to Sailor. "I can give the Elven a ride home."

The Elven?

Alessande was speechless. The last thing she wanted to do was get in a car with the vampire cop who was behaving as if she was a schoolgirl with no sense.

But before she could protest, Sailor said, "Mark, that would be great of you. Declan will be here soon—we're having dinner with a few of his shapeshifter friends, and it might be even more important now to see if any of them knows anything. Alessande is right up Mulholland Drive. I mean, I wouldn't mind at all, but since you offered..."

"No problem," Mark said. He smiled at Sailor, as if he felt real affection for her. She smiled back at him.

Great, Alessande thought. They were all just wonderful friends here. No doubt Declan Wainwright, a friend of Sailor's long before he'd fallen in love with her, also respected Mark Valiente.

If she turned the ride down, she would only appear to be unreasonable and unpleasant.

"Thank you," she said regally.

"I'll get her home," Mark said, "and then Brodie can meet me at the old Hildegard Studio and we'll check it out."

"I'll go with you," Alessande said.

Brodie protested. "What are you, Alessande? A glutton for punishment? I'll give Mark some time to get you home, and then he and I—and only he and I—will look around the studio. I understand what you're saying about the police, but Mark and I are not your usual cops."

Did it matter, she wondered, if she were there, so long as Brodie and Mark could help, if needed, while searching the place? She couldn't avoid feeling, however, that she had done the work; she was the one with the passion to save a life—and they were just taking over.

She determined not to waste time and energy arguing anymore.

"They took me yesterday—they meant me to be a sacrifice. But you—and they—underestimated my abilities. I would have gotten out. The thing is, I believe Regina was meant to die last night before they caught me snooping around. That means she's probably still alive. But for how long? We have to find her."

"We'll search the old studio thoroughly, Alessande," Brodie promised her. "If she's there, we'll find her."

"I doubt she's being held there any longer," Alessande said.

"Then we'll find the clues that will lead us to where she *is* being held. Not to mention that we arrested several people at the mausoleum," Brodie said.

"You already interrogated them for hours," Alessande said. "I know, because you kept me sitting there the whole time. Luckily I had some of your human colleagues to…talk to. Let's see, the tall 'dude' from Texas, along with his sister and girl-friend, claim to have met a man in a coffee shop who told them about a really cool role-playing ghost tour. Yeah, they were a lot of help. Then there was the junkie who didn't even know he'd been there. And last, the college student who had come to take photographs for the college paper to use for an article on old Hollywood. They were a *lot* of help."

"Someone has to know something," Mark said.

"You arrested five human beings. I doubt a human being is running things," Alessande told him.

"True enough. But right now we're looking for Regina," Mark replied. "And we're in a better position to do that than anyone else, even you, Alessande. You're not a one-woman army. We can help, so let us."

"All of us can help," Rhiannon told her.

"Help? The way you talk, only the police and Keepers are any use. Those of us who aren't part of those groups need to be good little Others and stay out of the way."

"Alessande, be reasonable. We need to act fast if we're going to break this case," Sailor said. "We need to bring all of the councils up to speed, make everyone in our community aware of what's going on, since it seems as if at least one rogue Other is involved."

We know that Others are involved, Alessande thought. She opened her mouth to say so, but Mark beat her to it.

"Sailor, Barrie, I believe that shapeshifters are involved and—"

Barrie interrupted him with a weary groan.

"And," Mark repeated, "perhaps vampires. I didn't see any Elven other than Alessande—though the Others in the congregation managed to disappear pretty quickly, and God knows a seasoned Elven can teleport in the blink of an eye. But I think it's possible that there's a conspiracy among those Others who resent the fact that the international council of Keepers is now working on establishing a universal legal code."

"We'll have to get in contact with the rest of the L.A.–area Keepers about this," Rhiannon said. "And we'll have to call our own councils to discuss the matter. Someone out there somewhere knows something. We just have to find out who."

"And anyone who's not equipped or trained to deal with criminal activity needs to stay out of it," Mark said, turning to look at Alessande.

She fought hard to control her temper.

Maybe it didn't help that he was so tall. As an Elven, she stood eye to eye with most men, but not him. Valiente was six foot four or so. He probably made a good cop. He was muscular and imposing, with ink-dark hair and the yellow-gold eyes that were frequently found among his kind, plus many striking features.

The better to terrify jaywalkers, she couldn't help but think.

"Shall we?" he offered.

She walked to the door and paused before turning back. "Brodie, if you and Mark are both going to the old studio, who's going to continue interrogating the humans you brought to the station?"

"Brodie already questioned them while you and I were speaking with the lieutenant," Mark told her. "Besides, you're the one who just said that they were basically worthless as sources of information."

"I know I did, but…didn't you learn anything? I couldn't hear everything that they were saying to Brodie," she said.

"Strange, it sounded like you did," Mark said casually.

"Most of them thought it was a show, something to amuse the tourists," Brodie explained. "The junkie said he thought he'd joined up with a religious group performing a ritual. Only thing he heard that impressed me was that he thinks they believed they could bring Sebastian Hildegard back to life—that he's a new messiah."

"And he thought nothing of an ostensibly unconscious woman lying on top of a sarcophagus?" Alessande asked.

"He thought you were part of the group, that you were just there to greet Sebastian when he came back to life," Brodie told her. "He thought the knives were merely symbolic."

"But—"

"We can't prove that he or any of them knew you

were kidnapped. They all seemed to believe that you were a volunteer, part of the ritual, the show, the tour—whatever they had stumbled into," Brodie said quietly.

Mark sighed. "We don't even have enough evidence to hold them for more than twenty-four hours. One guy threatened to sue the department for breaching his civil rights. Says even if he stumbled into something he knew nothing about, everyone is entitled to religious freedom. At least we interrupted the really bad guys tonight. Being Others, they were a lot more powerful and dangerous than the people we've got in custody. The sect, or whatever it is, is going to be regrouping."

They were getting nowhere, Alessande realized, and continued on toward the door. She turned once more, looking back at the Gryffald cousins. "Thank you," she told them.

With all the dignity she could muster, she stood by the door and waited for Mark. All she had to do now was keep a civil tongue until the vampire cop got her home so she could sleep for a while and forget the trauma—and the failure—of that night.

She had to admit, she was exhausted.

Mark Valiente joined her at the door, led her out and pointed to the vintage Mustang in the driveway. She already knew it was his car, although she had made the drive from the police station to the House of the Rising Sun with Brodie.

"Pretty nice car for a cop," she said, then wanted to bite her tongue. *Be civil,* she chastised herself.

He shrugged. "It moves when it needs to," he assured her, then grinned. "It's actually my work car—came out of a police auction."

The car didn't have much of a backseat, but the front seats were comfortable and afforded a lot of space for long legs. Alessande slid in quickly, before he could hold much less open the door for her, though she didn't know if he would have tried to or not.

They were both silent as he headed down the driveway, waited as the gate opened and eased out onto the road. It was dusk. The air was growing cooler, and the sun was falling in the western sky. The sunset was beautiful, shades of purple and orange slowly disappearing in the encroaching darkness. She couldn't believe how late it had gotten, but they'd been at the police station for what had seemed like forever after the raid at the tomb, and then they'd been at the House of the Rising Sun for a while, too.

Alessande turned, looking at him, and said at last, "What about the bad guys? Do you think they'll kill Regina out of anger over what happened—whether to get even with us or as a warning?"

"I don't think that Regina is in any more danger than she has been. She's Elven, young and very beautiful. I imagine they want her for something important," Mark responded. He glanced her way. "As an ancient, you should be able to tell me. Do you know anything firsthand about Sebastian Hildegard?"

There it was—that damned age reference again. "I was in Scotland at the time," she said haughtily. "What about you, vampire? How the hell old are you? Weren't you around at the time?"

He smiled grimly. "I was living in New York City back then. And," he said, assessing her, "what are you really? About eighty?"

"One hundred six."

"I was born soon after the American Civil War. I suppose I do have you by a few years. My family didn't come out to California until the 1970s. We moved around a lot before that. You know, you can't stay anywhere long when you don't age."

Alessande started to open her mouth as they were driving along the steep winding trail of Mulholland Drive, but something slammed down on the roof of the car—as if hit by the Hand of God. The Mustang veered wildly toward the edge of the cliff, teetering dangerously toward the chasm that plunged hundreds of feet to the ground—and certain death.

Chapter 2

Mark prided himself on being alert and wary of danger at all times, but the thunderous attack on the Mustang had taken him completely by surprise.

He gripped the wheel in a death lock and swung the car around, barely saving them from a fatal fall into the canyon below. As he jerked the car to a halt, he knew that something evil was out there with them on the road where the houses were few, far between and built into the cliff at all angles.

He looked over at Alessande; to her credit, she hadn't screamed, didn't seem to be in a panic and was staring at him as if ready to follow his lead.

"Go," he told her softly. "Teleport, but not home. Go back to the House of the Rising Sun."

"I can help—"

"Please…go. I think they're after you."

She didn't need to ask him why he had told her to return to the Gryffald estate. They both knew that teleporting took a vast amount of energy, and that she would be in a weakened state once she reached her goal, so the best place to be was among friends with supernatural strengths of their own.

He got a good look at her in the split second when she nodded before teleporting.

She really was stunning. Of course the Elven came that way. But her face was as perfect as a fairy-tale princess, her eyes as deep and mercurial and enchanting as the sea, and the spun white-gold of her hair framed her classic features.

Then she was gone.

And when he looked up, a giant eagle was ripping the roof off his car.

Shapeshifter!

At least Alessande had listened to him; she was gone, and she would be safe.

As the top of his car went flying over the canyon, Mark leaped out. He was excellent at transformation himself; in an instant he was airborne in the guise of a vampire bat. After a few seconds of intense concentration, he had increased his own size to that of the eagle. Flying ever upward, he avoided the sharp talons of his foe. Soaring above the gargantuan bird, he dive-bombed and caught the thing at the back of the neck, careful to hold it without inflicting a crucial bite.

But even as he did his best not to kill it, he rued his own stupidity in getting this close to an Other with this size and power.

It must have taken a lot for the shapeshifter to become such a mammoth creature, but it hadn't been the end of the shifter's strength. Now the thing turned into a gnat and slipped easily out of Mark's grasp.

Swearing, he concentrated on his own body, shrinking, then changing back into his human form. He stood next to his car, staring with disgust at the ruined vehicle.

He'd lost his attacker.

And he'd lost his car. Materialistic and shallow as it might be, he had loved that car.

He swore, dug his cell phone out of his pocket and called Brodie. "Did Alessande make it back all right?" he asked anxiously.

"Yes, she's here," Brodie told him. "She's exhausted, though. Sailor has given her tea and gotten her up to bed. What happened? Did you catch him? Alessande said it was as if a two-ton crane smacked down on the car."

"Shapeshifter, definitely," Mark said. "And no, I was trying to keep it alive, so—thanks to my own stupidity—it went into gnat form and disappeared. You're sure that Alessande is all right?"

"Yes, she's fine. She really needs sleep. It's a good thing she's in exceptional shape—eats the right food, exercises, hones her skills to perfection—because the last twenty-four hours have taken a lot out of her.

I'll call impound and let them know the car needs to be towed in. I'm sure they'll want to know what the hell happened to it. Is it fixable?"

Mark looked at his car. "No," he said sadly. Still on the phone, he walked over to it. With an angry shove of his foot, he used his supernatural strength and sent it over the edge, crashing down into the bracken in the valley below.

"Don't worry about the car. I got rid of it. It would have been too hard to explain. Come get me—I'm about two miles away on Mulholland—and we'll head to the old studio, check it out, see what we can find."

"Be there in five," Brodie told him.

As Mark waited for Brodie's arrival, he was worried, really worried. Someone knew that Alessande was on to something.

And that someone seriously wanted her out of the way.

"I know it's nothing like your house, Alessande," Sailor said apologetically as she got her friend settled. "I mean, Castle House is kind of Goth-gone-bad compared to your place. But it's safer for you to stay here."

Alessande was comfortably stretched out on the bed in the guest room, with the cousins keeping her company. She hadn't had much strength when she had started to teleport, already exhausted from everything she'd been through, so she'd more or less crash-landed on the Castle House stairs, startling everyone who was still there. And before Sailor had led her up here, they'd been talking about her staying for days, maybe even weeks—and they hadn't bothered consulting her. Worst of all, Mark Valiente wasn't even around for her to blame anything on.

"You drank enough water, right?" Sailor asked, breaking into Alessande's thoughts.

Teleporting could dehydrate the body to a dangerous extent. Alessande had consumed nearly a gallon of water since she'd arrived.

"I'm good, thank you," she said.

"Alessande, we believe that you're marked for extinction," Brodie said firmly as he stepped into the room.

She shook her head, wanting to deny the possibility. "Have you heard from Mark?" she asked. He was a jerk, but he was the jerk who had worried about her safety first. And she'd never experienced anything like the feel of being in that car when it was attacked by a ten-ton taloned *something*.

"I'm on my way to get him," Brodie said. He looked at Sailor. "You all sit tight and be careful. I don't know if they will dare to attack this place, or if they've exhausted their resources for another night."

Barrie, sitting in a chair by the window, rose. "I've got to call an emergency meeting of the shapeshifters. I know it's a rogue individual or group behind this—most of my Others would be horrified by what's happening."

Rhiannon, rising from the foot of the bed, set a hand on Barrie's shoulder. "Barrie, don't take this on as if the weight of the world is yours and yours alone. We all know that Others, no matter what their race, are just like people. Most are law abiding and want nothing more than to lead good lives with decent people around them. No one is going to think that all shapeshifters are bad. We know better in this day and age."

"And," Declan said, walking into the room, "no meeting tonight, Barrie." He walked over to stand behind Sailor, setting his hands on her shoulders. "I just talked to Mark. He wants people here, keeping Alessande safe tonight. I'll stay with the women. Brodie, you and Mark can rest assured that everyone here will be protected while you check out the studio."

"What about the Snake Pit?" Barrie asked Declan.

Declan owned one of the hottest nightspots in the city. It was very popular with the Others, especially vampires. Since Declan was a shapeshifter Keeper, they often stayed to enjoy it after-hours, when only Others were welcome. But the rest of the time both locals and tourists were free to enjoy themselves there. Declan had a talent for getting the next up-and-coming bands to play, and Rhiannon, who was a singer as well as a Keeper, performed there regularly. She also performed at the Mystic Café, where her boss was a werewolf Keeper.

"The Snake Pit can survive one night without me," Declan said firmly.

Jonquil was waiting at the foot of the bed. He barked as if to reaffirm Declan's statement.

"I'll follow you down in a minute and lock the door behind you," Sailor said. "The compound will be safe. Jonquil knows better than any alarm when someone gets near Castle House."

"Don't forget Wizard," Rhiannon said. "He guards the grounds like a hellhound. We'll be all right."

Wizard did look like a hellhound, Alessande reflected. He was a mix of Scottish deerhound and something else humongous. If anyone even looked cross-eyed at Rhiannon, Wizard would take them down in a heartbeat.

Rhiannon left the room, presumably to give Wizard his instructions, and Barrie rose, as well. "Get some rest," she told Alessande. "I'm going online to read the news reports and try to get a better grip on this."

Sailor patted Alessande's pillow. "Can I get you anything else?" she asked.

"I have tea and a lovely bed, and I'm being protected by some of the finest women in L.A., a ghost and two ferocious dogs. I feel like a hothouse flower," Alessande admitted.

Sailor grinned. "Uncomfortable for you, I know. But even Achilles had his damned heel. I learned— with a lot of help from you—to handle responsibility and be brave. Now, from me, you can learn to trust in others and let them be your strength sometimes."

Alessande smiled and nodded. "Okay. I think I'll try to sleep. That teleporting thing is...draining."

It was. Sailor left her, telling Jonquil to stay and stand watch, and Alessande found herself falling almost instantly to sleep.

It was strange, though. She was asleep, yet she still seemed to be aware of her surroundings. At first she knew that she was in bed in the guest room at Castle House. But then the bed seemed to grow hard beneath her, and the dust motes dancing in the air turned into a mixture of ash and fog.

She could hear music, something from an old movie she had caught on cable. She couldn't quite place it, though—and then she did. It was from Franco Zeffirelli's version of *Romeo and Juliet*.

There was movement all around her. She wanted to rise and see what was going on, but she couldn't. Something was weighing her down, refusing to let her up.

The music was beautiful, and she tried to open her eyes. She managed to raise her lids far enough to see that she seemed to be in a church. There was a wedding going on, she thought. The Gryffald cousins were there, standing around where she lay. Handsome men in tuxes were seating the guests, and she saw that Father Gunderson—an Elven himself—was ready to officiate at the ceremony.

She couldn't turn her head, but she caught sight of the long white sleeve on her arm.

She was wearing a wedding dress.

It was *her* wedding!

But something was very wrong. She should have been walking down the aisle, not lying on the altar. And everyone was beginning to scream in horror and shout to one another. And above all the noise, she could hear one voice.

It was the vampire cop. Mark Valiente. And he was screaming her name as if…as if he thought that if he shouted loudly enough he could wake her and save her from the horror that was about to take place.

Warned by his shouting, she realized that she had to break free from whatever was holding her there, frozen to the altar. She managed to turn her head and saw the red velvet runner than stretched from the altar to the door. Except that it wasn't a runner. It was a river of blood.

She jerked herself awake. She was in the guest bedroom at Castle House. She'd had a nightmare and nothing more.

It was night, and she was safe…. She closed her eyes again.

She could hear the cousins and Declan Wainwright talking downstairs. They were joined by another male voice: Mick Townsend, Barrie's love— and a shapeshifter.

Shapeshifters, vampires… Were more of the Other races involved in the evil, as well? Leprechauns, gnomes, weres?

Elven?

No, she couldn't believe that the male Elven

population would ever accept the sacrifice of Elven women. Her own people couldn't be involved.

She hadn't realized that she was prejudiced before all this began, but the truth was, she did think of her kind as more ethical, far less violent, and...a cut above.

"Wrong," she murmured.

The truth was that Elven *could* be involved; she had to acknowledge that. Evil was evil—and it came in all guises.

Just as *good* came in all forms. She had to accept help and be grateful—and learn not to judge.

Jonquil whined and licked her fingers. "Good dog," she told him.

She lay there, knowing that she desperately needed rest, but she was afraid to sleep again, afraid of her dreams. She was tempted to run downstairs so that she could be with people.

Jonquil whined softly again. He nudged her hand and wagged his tail.

The dog was with her, standing guard so closely, she dared to shut her eyes again.

And when she slept next, it was deeply.

Mark and Brodie pulled up two blocks from the old Hildegard Studio.

They weren't there on official police business. Alessande had been right about one thing: to be official, they would need a search warrant. They didn't have that kind of time.

They went through the hole in the gate that Alessande had told them about, rather than using their powers. Mark was only at half strength, having used up his reserves becoming a giant bat earlier. And it would just be a waste of energy he might need later should Brodie need to teleport and Mark make one more transformation into a bat.

There were five long soundstages that comprised the studio. Abandoned and neglected, they were dark and dangerous. Brodie had come prepared with large flashlights so they could see their way around.

They went cautiously and methodically from one stage to the next. The first three were empty, and it didn't appear that anyone had been there for years. Cameras, lighting, sets, props—nothing remained.

The fourth soundstage was different.

The last thing filmed in it might well have been during the 1940s. Huge old cameras stood sentinel, along with recording equipment that could have housed elephants. Two sets remained; one was a cemetery at night. Walking around it, they found cardboard headstones, rubber hatchets and plastic guns and knives. There were fake corpses sticking out of graves—most of them truly rotting by this point.

Brodie found a film marker. "It was called *The Awakening of Dr. Evil.* A classic, I'm sure. Did you ever see it?"

"Can't say that I caught it," Mark told him.

The second set was equally sad—like something

lost in time. It was also filthy and decaying. "I'm surprised all this wasn't broken down, like on the other soundstages. With the cost of things these days, I would think someone would snap this place up and start a new studio. Everything here is outdated," Brodie said.

"Yeah, but…just the real estate."

"True," Brodie agreed.

"I wonder if the dead women were ever here, or whether the killer—or killers—hid here, sneaking out to snatch the women as they passed by," Mark said thoughtfully.

"Doesn't seem that we've found anything to give us that answer yet," Brodie said.

"Anyway, we have one more soundstage to go," Mark reminded him.

They headed to the fifth building.

Like the fourth, it had not been completely stripped. This set looked as if it had been meant for a Victorian-era film. The facades of houses decorated with gingerbread porches and window trim stood to one side, while the other half of the soundstage had been dressed to resemble a series of businesses from the same time period. One of them had a huge sign that read Wax Works! Enter if Ye Dare!

"Hildegard seems to have been doing a lot of horror movies," Brodie commented.

"Maybe he was living a horror movie," Mark said. "I don't really know anything about him, other than that he was a famous magician."

"He booked himself as 'Sebastian the Magnificent,'" Brodie said. "I remember one of my dad's old friends talking about him one night when my father first took me to the House of Illusion. He was good—today he'd be all over TV, I imagine. But Sebastian also loved movies—making them, that is—and I imagine that's why he founded the studio. But onstage, he was pretty amazing." He paused and looked at Mark. "He liked to tell the crowds that he could even defy death."

"As far as I know, he's been buried for years," Mark said.

"*Has* been buried…"

"Apparently now someone wants to see if the illusionist really *can* defy death," Mark said.

"So—do we start with the Hildegard family?" Brodie asked.

"As good a place as any," Mark said. He walked over to the wax works, aiming his flashlight as he went.

Behind the facade he saw a love seat with a script on it. Moving closer, he noticed that there was no dust on the wood or upholstery—or the end table next to it.

He slipped on a latex glove and picked up the script. He flipped it over to read the title aloud. "*Death in the Bowery,* by Greg Swayze." It was new, by an up-and-coming scriptwriter whose name Mark thought he recognized. He looked up as Brodie joined him. "Someone's been here," he said. "Could be Swayze himself, or maybe someone else with access to his script."

"Is he an Other? I don't know the name," Brodie said.

"He's fairly new to L.A. I don't know—we can ask the women if they've heard about him. Sailor's in the business, so she might know," Mark said.

L.A. was a hard place to be a Keeper, he reflected. Someone was always shooting a horror movie somewhere in town, and that made it very difficult to discern the real from the feigned.

Truth from illusion.

"Just because the guy's screenplay is here doesn't make him guilty. One or both of the dead women might have been an aspiring actress. They could have been given a copy to read, and they might even have been lured here on the pretext of an audition," Brodie said.

"Newcomers to the area—yeah, they might have been here for the Hollywood dream," Mark said. "We could go back to the station and find out about our murder victims, and then have a visit with the reigning Hildegard." He grimaced. "Ah, hell. I forgot that I have to go in and do paperwork over the car incident."

"I reported that someone drove you off the road, and that you barely escaped with your life," Brodie told him. "I bought us the time to do this, but, yeah—the lieutenant is going to want a report."

"Paperwork," Mark groaned.

"Happens to the best of us," Brodie said. "Let's head on out. We didn't find anyone—but so far no one has found *us,* either."

Alessande awoke to the gentle touch of a hand on her shoulder. She expected Sailor or Rhiannon or Barrie. She jerked when she saw the face of an elderly man.

Merlin!

"I'm so, so sorry, my dear. I didn't mean to startle you. You were whimpering in your sleep. I knocked, but you didn't answer, so… But I didn't wish to scare you."

Merlin was an extremely polite ghost. He'd been a lovely man in life, and he was a lovely man in death.

Without being an Other, he'd been a spectacular magician.

"It's okay, Merlin," she said quickly. "You just surprised me. I was whimpering? I had no idea. I thought I was out like a light."

"The mind is a mysterious machine, my dear," he said. "May I?" he asked, indicating the chair near the window.

"Of course."

Merlin was a talented ghost. He'd learned to use his ectoplasmic strength to great effect. He drew the chair over to her bedside and sat. "I've just heard about the events at the Hildegard tomb."

She winced. "Merlin, I've listened to a dozen lectures already."

"Oh, I'm not here to lecture you, Alessande."

"Thank you."

"I'm here to warn you," he said gravely.

"About?"

"Sebastian Hildegard," he said.

She frowned at that. "Sebastian Hildegard must be pretty well decayed by now—even if he was embalmed. Dead and buried, as they say. It's his heirs—or whoever is using his tomb—that we need to fear."

Merlin shook his head. She smiled, watching him. He was white-headed and distinguished; he would have made the perfect grandfather.

"No, you don't understand. I *knew* Sebastian Hildegard. He wasn't just an illusionist and a shapeshifter—he was a man dedicated to achieving immortality."

"But he's dead."

He shook his head at her naïveté. "Perhaps he *can* be resurrected. *He* certainly thought so."

Alessande chose her words carefully. "Merlin, we're all aware of the different powers we have, but even vampires can die. And shapeshifters don't have the life span that vampires do. Shapeshifters die."

"Sebastian *did* die," Merlin said. "Look, I know this is hard to believe, but it's true. Sebastian was into the occult—he studied ancient texts from dawn to dusk. I believe that part of him is still…is still in the atmosphere. Caught somewhere in time and space. And I believe that this cult intends to use the deaths of more young women to bring him back to life."

"Merlin, I just can't believe that's possible," Alessande said.

"Does it really matter if it's possible so long as people *believe* it's possible?"

Alessande murmured, "I guess not. So we should start by talking with his heirs, right?"

Merlin wagged a finger at her. "Not you, my dear. The police. The *police* need to start with the family."

"Merlin..."

"Alessande, you've angered the wrong people. You need to stay safe."

"I can't sit around when a girl is missing."

"You feel sorry for her," Merlin said. "And it makes you feel that you need to get involved. Forgive me—I have been eavesdropping. I know what you did."

"I really *am* capable, Merlin. I just wanted to see who was behind the mask before I acted. If I could have gotten to the truth, I—"

"What truth, Alessande? You're dealing with *shapeshifters*. You could have seen anyone—a young mother. A politician. A—"

She shook her head. "Under the mask and cowl, the leader was showing his—or her—true face. I'm sure of it."

"Maybe. And maybe not. He—or she—got away, right?"

"So you suggest that I just sit here and do nothing?"

"Yes."

Alessande sat up. "Merlin, I don't intend to endanger anyone else, but I won't just sit here. When the Celebrity Virus went around, every single Elven out there was susceptible—and the only way to stop it was to go out and do something. I won't spend the rest of my life being afraid."

She was startled to see that he was leaning away from her in his chair and staring at her strangely.

"What?" she demanded.

"You, uh, you've changed," he told her.

"What are you talking about?" she asked sharply.

He indicated the mirror. She hopped from the bed and walked over to the guest room's full-length swivel mirror...

...where she stared at her own reflection and gasped softly.

Chapter 3

Mark Valiente figured they were incredibly lucky that Bryce Edwards, a very, very old werewolf, had been transferred over to become their lieutenant in the robbery homicide division. He'd been in Vice for many years, but after some of the recent disturbances in the Otherworld, he'd finessed a transfer.

They didn't take long at the station. They explained what had happened, and Bryce put in a requisition for Mark to get another car.

"I'd been expecting you earlier," Lieutenant Edwards told them. The werewolf looked like someone's grandfather or a lean, beardless version of Santa Claus. But he was sharp, and he was in the right position, because he knew the law, people—and Others—through and through. "But now I see what caused the delay." He studied Mark. "Pretty lucky you were able to fight him off. Were you seen?"

"The good thing is, if we were and someone called it in, 911 would just chalk it up to a movie being filmed or an overdose of something at a Hollywood party," Mark told him. "Why? Any wacky calls to the station?"

"No, except for the one I'm about to get to—which wasn't wacky, just preemptive," Edwards said. He slid over a piece of paper. "Alan Hildegard called—he's representing his kin. Naturally he was extremely disturbed to hear that his family's vault was used by 'such maniacs' for their evil purposes. He wants to cooperate with the police in any and every way possible in regard to shutting down this occult group dedicated to raising his great-grandfather from the grave."

"Alan Hildegard," Mark mused. "He's running the family interests now? Aren't there several brothers, sisters and cousins?"

Edwards shrugged. "Alan is the self-professed head of the family. The oldest son of the oldest son or whatever. He owns the estate. I think one of the sisters lives there, too, and maybe their cousin. I thanked him for his cooperation and told him you were on your way or would be soon. He's expecting you."

"Lieutenant," Mark said, "we found a screenplay on one of the old soundstages—a new screenplay. We're going to go and see the author, Greg Swayze—

because who knows what it was doing there. He could be involved. At the very least, maybe he has some insight. Additionally, now that it's been confirmed that Others are involved, we'd like to take over as lead detectives on the murders of Leesa Adair and Judith Belgrave." He leaned forward. "The media has speculated about a serial killer, of course, but we—the police—haven't made an official statement. However, with what we know now…it seems that these deaths were at the hand of the same killer or killers. There's a young Elven woman missing still, and we're racing against time, hoping to find her before it's too late. Were Adair and Belgrave here for the Hollywood dream? Would they have been actively auditioning? We need to know this stuff, and it will be a lot easier if they're our cases."

"Way ahead of you." Edwards picked up two files from his desk and opened one. "Leesa Adair, twenty-nine, graduate of Carnegie Mellon's theater school." He flipped open the other folder. "Judith Belgrave was a waitress in Ramsay, New Jersey, before picking up and heading out here. Hang on, let me check the family interviews…." He skimmed through the file and then looked up at them. "She told her sister she planned on being discovered. Said that in acting, a degree was a bunch of bull—you could act or not, and if you got the break, you could learn while doing. The camera would like you or it wouldn't. So, yes, it seems that both girls were here following the age-old Hollywood dream."

"And," Brodie said, "Regina and Alessande met on a film set, so—"

"So someone seems to be targeting actresses," Edwards said. "But things aren't always what they seem," he warned them. "The percentages of actresses out here is sky-high. Every waitress you meet is an actress—along with every female bartender and half the hotel clerks."

"Yes, but the women's descriptions…" Mark said, remembering the briefing they'd all received on the cases. "Tall, blonde and blue- or green-eyed."

Elven or Elven-looking *actresses.*

"All right, well…I'll speak with Harvey Olstein and Myra McQueen, and get both cases transferred over to you. I don't think they'll mind. They've got plenty of other cases on their plates. Then I'll call over to Missing Persons and tell them you're pretty sure that the murders and the disappearance need to be seen as a serial event. Homicide feels they're at a dead end as far as clues go, and Missing Persons has followed every lead, as well. No one knew about the old Hildegard Studio until you two walked in."

"We didn't know about it until we took Alessande to the House of the Rising Sun and got to talking," Brodie explained.

Edwards shook his head. "And that girl was in here—being interviewed—half the night and morning!"

"In her defense, Lieutenant, I don't think she knew the head of Robbery Homicide is an old werewolf," Brodie said. "She wouldn't have known to ask to speak with you."

"*Old* werewolf?" Edwards demanded.

"*Experienced* werewolf," Mark said quickly.

"Humph," Edwards said. "Get going, then. Oh, and, Mark, you can pick up another car tomorrow. I've asked the auction guys to scrounge around for something you'll like—can't guarantee another vintage Mustang, though."

Mark nodded. "Yeah, well...hey. It's just a car, right?" He knew that Brodie was laughing at him. Too bad. He really did like vintage Mustangs.

"We'll go to the Hildegard estate," Brodie said.

"You'd better get this one solved quickly," Edwards told them. He shook his head. "I hate it when Others cause trouble. So messy. Damn." He pointed a finger at them. "Move it!"

By the time the Gryffald cousins, accompanied by Declan Wainwright and Mick Townsend, made it up to the guest room in response to Alessande's summons, the "change" that had taken place had already diminished.

"I'm completely confused," Barrie said. "You *changed?* Into what?"

"A giant! An angry giant!" Merlin exclaimed.

"Elven don't shift," Sailor said flatly.

"You *are* Elven, right?" Rhiannon demanded.

"You know I'm Elven!" Alessande said. "And I didn't change into an angry giant."

"Okay, so—" Barrie continued.

"Angry giant," Merlin insisted.

"All right, I'm worried—obviously, or I wouldn't have called you up here. I…got bigger," Alessande admitted.

"Fat?" Sailor asked.

"No—all of me. I was about seven feet tall…and I did look a little peeved," Alessande said.

Declan spoke softly. "Baby shapeshifters and occasionally even shapeshifter Keepers do it sometimes," he said softly. "When they're hungry, scared…they suddenly appear bigger. Not giant, but…bigger," he repeated. "As infants, they can't control their shifting."

They were all staring at her. "I'm not a shifter! I remember my mother, and she was Elven."

"But your father died when you were very young," Barrie said. "Are you just as sure about *him?*"

"Stop staring at me, all of you. I feel like a sideshow at the circus," Alessande said.

"If we have children," Sailor said, looking at Declan, "they'll be…mixed."

"Mixed Keeper—fairly common," Declan said.

"Who was your father?" Rhiannon asked speculatively. "If he were a shifter Keeper, that might explain why you never showed the ability until now. Think about it. Every living creature—human, Other, animal—gets a quarter of his or her DNA from each grandparent. Sometimes a brown-eyed parent and a blue-eyed parent have a blue-eyed baby, and sometimes they have a brown-eyed one. And sometimes our Otherworldly powers come out later in life," Rhiannon said.

"She can't be half Keeper," Barrie said. "She's Elven—we all know Elven when we see one. Besides, if she'd been born to be a Keeper, she'd have the birthmark," Barrie said. "We're all born with the mark of the race we'll grow up to manage and whose talents we'll share."

"There! I have no birthmark!" Alessande said. "And I'm *not* stripping to prove it."

Declan laughed. Mick, a shapeshifter himself, studied Alessande. "Half-breed," he told her. "You must have the mark somewhere. Somewhere you don't see."

They all stared at her as she insisted, "Hey, I meant it. No pat downs, no body inspections."

"Where do people never see themselves?" Rhiannon asked, looking at Barrie.

"Um, the butt?" Barrie suggested.

"Stop!" Alessande protested.

Rhiannon laughed. "I wasn't thinking of anything quite so—well, quite so whatever. I was thinking the bottoms of the feet."

"It wouldn't be too intimate or personal a question if we were to ask to see the bottoms of your feet, would it?" Declan teased.

"Knock yourselves out," Alessande said, sitting at the foot of the bed and lifting her legs.

They all stared.

And then they looked into her eyes.

"What?" Alessande cried.

"Shapeshifter," Barrie said softly. "You may be Elven, but you were also born to be a Keeper for the shapeshifter community."

"She's right. It's faint, but the mark is there," Declan said.

They all backed away, still staring at her. "Your mother never told you that your father was a shapeshifter Keeper?" Sailor asked her.

"No! I thought it wasn't even acceptable for Others to…well, you know, have relationships with different races of Others until just recently," Alessande said.

"Acceptable or not, I'm sure it's happened throughout time," Rhiannon told them. "People have always intermingled—whether it was socially acceptable or not."

"And," Sailor added thoughtfully, "while we may all want to believe we've magically become open-minded, the play *Avenue Q* has it right. Everyone is a little bit racist."

Alessande winced, her lashes veiling her eyes. Yes, she admitted to herself, it was true. She herself had been down on Mark Valiente for being a vampire.

"Do you think they hid their relationship, afraid of what other…*Others* might think?" Barrie asked.

"My mother died when I was seven. Maybe she

meant to tell me when I was older," Alessande said. "Maybe she didn't want me knowing—afraid of how I'd be accepted in the Elven world if I let it slip."

"If you think about it, this is really a great thing," Barrie said. "You have the power of the Elven and the power of shifting, too."

"I can't shape-shift. Whatever happened was a total accident. And that's bad—really bad," Alessande said.

"No, we'll work on it. You need to practice, learn to concentrate," Mick told her.

"You have Mick, Declan and me. We'll help you," Barrie assured her.

Alessande looked at them. And then the magnitude of what was happening slowly swept over her. She hadn't known how to mind read or teleport as a small child; she'd learned from her mother and then from her stepparents. It was like learning to walk, to talk....

"You won't *be* a shapeshifter," Mick said.

"You'll still be Elven," Sailor assured her.

"You're just destined to be a Keeper, as well," Rhiannon said.

"Which means that you can master the ability to shift," Barrie assured her.

And if she could do that, Alessande thought, how much more effective would she be to enter the world of illusionists—and the bizarre cult that had grown up around Sebastian Hildegard?

* * *

The Hildegard estate was a relic of old Hollywood, set on a hill and guarded by heavy iron gates—much like the House of the Rising Sun.

Sebastian Hildegard had built the place with materials brought over from the Bavarian section of Germany and had filled it with antiques from the same region. It looked like a truly Gothic version of one of Mad King Ludwig's fairy-tale castles.

As Brodie maneuvered the car toward the drive, his phone rang. "Rhiannon," he told Mark briefly, pulling over to take the call. He frowned as he listened, occasionally asking cryptic questions. "Really?...Is that possible?...What does it mean?"

When he hung up, he was silent.

"Well?" Mark demanded.

"It's Alessande."

"Is she all right?" Mark asked, wondering why his heart had started pounding so suddenly when he found her to be such a nuisance.

"She's fine. She—she changed."

"Changed clothes? Changed religions? Political parties? What do you mean, *she changed?*"

Brodie turned to stare at him. "Apparently she was talking to Merlin and became very upset. When she did, she suddenly grew a foot taller and looked like an angry giant—Merlin's words, according to Rhiannon. Anyway, they discovered a birthmark on her foot."

"What?" Mark demanded. *Keepers* were born

with birthmarks. "The woman is Elven. I've never seen anyone who looks so Elven in my whole life."

Brodie nodded. "I know, but…she's mixed."

"She can't be," Mark argued. "It was forbidden until this generation. The Others barely got along with each breed, which is surely why the Ultimate Power—God, if you want—created Keepers. We Others can be nasty bloodthirsty monsters when we're not kept in check."

"So can human beings," Brodie reminded him. "Anyway, Alessande never knew her real father, because he died when she was a baby. Her mother remarried, and then her mother and her stepfather died—"

"I know that. And I'm sure that's why she feels so responsible for Regina," Mark said.

"The point is, she didn't know her father. And the evidence says he must have been a shifter Keeper."

Mark mulled that over. "She won't know what she's doing," he said quietly. "This could mean even more trouble for her."

"A Keeper's job *is* trouble," Brodie reminded him.

"But she's not a Keeper—yet. Not really. A Keeper is assigned to a certain area. Rhiannon is the Keeper of—"

"The canyon, yes," Brodie finished for him. "But there are all kinds of areas around L.A. where she might belong. Or maybe she's meant to be somewhere else altogether. Only time will tell."

This isn't good; it isn't good at all, Mark thought. *The woman is already headstrong and...*

"Let's get through this, then we'll head back to the House of the Rising Sun," Brodie said.

He pulled the car into the Hildegard drive and announced the two of them into the guardhouse speaker. A moment later the giant iron gates swung open. They navigated the long drive and parked in front of the house.

Mark stared up at the facade. It was a fitting home for a line of illusionists—and shapeshifters. It was like Cinderella's castle gone over to the dark side. Giant gargoyles sat guard above the porch and window ledges.

The day itself seemed to darken as they rang the bell.

A butler admitted them.

Human, Mark thought.

They were led down a dark hallway with ancient chandeliers and stands with armor from the fourteenth to the eighteenth centuries. A doorway led to the study where Alan Hildegard was waiting to speak with them.

He seemed to be a surprisingly small man, but then Brodie was Elven and six foot four, and Mark, though a vampire, was his equal in height.

Mark had known the Hildegard name most of his life. His mother had been a working character actress, and she still emerged from her Arizona retirement now and then to play someone's mother or grandmother. He'd grown up hearing about the famous inhabitants of L.A.

He knew all the legends about old Sebastian Hildegard. He'd just never had occasion to be at the Hildegard estate or meet the current generation.

Alan Hildegard did not fit the house, and not only because he was slight. He was in a navy blue suit that made him look like a stockbroker. He was about five foot eleven and had sandy hair. While his clothing gave him the appearance of a businessman, his casual haircut and deep tan made him look like a surf bum gone Wall Street.

Shapeshifter, most likely, Mark presumed, given the Hildegard lineage.

"Good to see you—I've been waiting for L.A.'s finest," he told them, offering his hand to each man in turn.

"Yes, thank you for seeing us," Mark told him. "I'm Detective Mark Valiente, and this is Detective Brodie McKay."

"Can I get you gentlemen something? I realize you're on duty, so…coffee? Water? A soda?"

"I could definitely go for coffee," Brodie said.

"Sure. Have a seat. I'll call Jimmy, and he'll take care of us," Hildegard told them.

He indicated a group of chairs arranged on three sides of a lion-legged coffee table that faced a giant tiled and marble hearth. They sat while Hildegard moved to a phone on a side table and spoke with Jimmy.

Then, flipping the tails of his jacket, Hildegard joined them.

"I understand that a group of…thugs has been using my family tomb for some brand of cult nonsense," he said, irritated. "And that you two broke them up and got them the hell out of there—something for which I'm eternally grateful. I can't believe that the family sold off the cemetery—before my time, I assure you. It's disgraceful."

"We caught a number of people—but, sad to say, none of them were the ringleaders," Mark said. "They claimed there wasn't going to be a sacrifice, that—"

"I don't care! Charge them with trespassing. With desecrating a grave," Hildegard said impatiently. "I want them jailed. We may not own the cemetery any longer, but we have a contract that guarantees perpetual care of the family vault."

"Mr. Hildegard—" Mark began.

"Vampire, right?" Hildegard demanded suddenly.

"Yes."

"And Elven?" he asked, turning to Brodie.

"Yes," Brodie told him.

"At least this time I don't have to mess with idiot human beings who have no idea what they're up against with some of these—creatures!"

"A werewolf runs our robbery homicide division," Brodie told him.

"Yeah, I talked to him today. I was impressed," Hildegard said.

"All right, well, we don't mean to be offensive in any way," Mark said, "but, you understand, we have to ask you some questions."

"Me?" Hildegard didn't appear to be offended, just surprised. "I certainly wasn't there when my family's vault was being so shamefully used."

"I understand that," Mark said. "But it's become clear that someone out there is making use of your great-grandfather's legend. They've put together some kind of cross-species blood cult—there were human beings, shapeshifters, vampires… We're not sure just how many Other races were involved."

"They worship Sebastian Hildegard's memory and are convinced they can raise him from the grave to be some kind of god," Brodie said.

"Trust me," Hildegard said, and he grinned, "I'm not behind any faction that wants to make a god out of my great-grandfather. I like being the head of the family."

"You are in the magic business, aren't you?" Brodie asked.

Hildegard laughed at that. "No—or rather, only in the typical Hollywood sense. I'm a producer. I put together packages for that new cable channel—Horrific. They've just started airing original movies, although we're still pulling cheapies from the studio vaults, mostly." He gave them a wry look that made his opinion of those cheapies quite clear. "Next original—*Slasher and the Sleaze*. Thing is, you can make those pictures ridiculously cheaply, and they sell like hotcakes on DVD all around the world."

"So, these movies you're producing," Brodie said, "are you using the old family studio at all?"

Alan Hildegard's features tightened as if he'd just been attacked by a sudden jolt of extreme indigestion.

"As you know, the fate of the studio is still in dispute," he said angrily. "It's the land I want. Nothing on those old soundstages is worth two cents. The equipment is older than Moses. No, Horrific has brand-new, state-of-the-art soundstages in Universal City. And I don't really like hanging around the studio all day anyway. I'm a moneyman. I invest my own funds in prime projects and raise more as needed—and I confess I like wielding power. I love having the right and the ability to fire idiots at will." He glanced at Brodie and half smiled, tilting his head at a curious angle. "That's where I've seen you before—you were an actor! I saw you on stage in—"

Brodie shook his head firmly. "I was undercover at the time. I'm not an actor. I'm a cop. I like being a cop. I'm good at it. It's what I was born to be."

"Then you understand how I feel," Hildegard said. "When you're born a Hildegard, everyone thinks you have to be a magician. Well, I'm not. So, back to the vault. Just why were you there, if you don't mind my asking?"

"The department received an anonymous tip," Mark said, "and we went in to investigate. We discovered a young woman, who we later found out had been kidnapped, being held captive and apparently unconscious on top of your great-grandfather's sarcophagus. We believe that the head priest or whatever he calls himself was going to sacrifice her in the mistaken belief that her death could bring Sebastian back to life."

"Thank God you saved her," Hildegard said.

"Mr. Hildegard," Brodie said, leaning forward. "Two women mysteriously disappeared in what we believe was the vicinity of your old family studio and later showed up dead. Another woman is missing in similar circumstances. If you can think of anyone who might believe they can bring your great-grandfather back to life or is simply fixated on him in some way, we're on a desperate hunt to find the missing girl before she, too, winds up dead."

Hildegard looked confused. "This is L.A. County. It's sad, but women come here all the time, drawn by the desire for fame. And even sadder, some of them die. We do have crime—despite your best efforts."

As he spoke, a woman suddenly came sweeping into the room. She was small, perhaps five-two or five-three, slim, well built and very pretty, with huge blue eyes and golden-blond hair worn to her shoulders.

"Alan! Jimmy told me that the police were here." She paused, looking at Brodie and Mark, who both rose.

"My sister, Brigitte," Alan Hildegard said. "Brigitte, these are Detectives Mark Valiente and Brodie McKay."

Brodie and Mark both murmured polite greetings.

She walked over and shook hands with a surprisingly strong grip for someone so small. "Are you here about that awful business in the cemetery?" she asked.

"Yes," Mark said.

"I do hope you catch and prosecute those—*defilers* to the full extent of the law," she said.

"The detectives believe we have a bigger problem, my dear," Alan Hildegard said. "Two women have died—and another is missing. Their fates seem to have something to do with the fool who's creating a religion around Great-Grandfather."

Brigitte looked at Mark and Brodie in horror. "Someone is killing people over *Sebastian?* How horrible—and ridiculous. But…what makes you think there's a link to Sebastian?"

Mark and Brodie didn't look at one another; they both knew they had no intention of explaining anything about Alessande's involvement.

"I'm afraid we can't go into the details of an ongoing investigation," Mark said.

"I'm sure you understand," Brodie added.

"So why on earth do you think we can help?" Brigitte asked.

"Perhaps someone has been hounding your family—or maybe bothering you for details about Sebastian that only the family might know," Mark said.

Just then Jimmy came into the room carrying a silver tray. "Coffee, sir," he told Alan.

He set the tray on the table before the fire, turned and left.

"Sit down, please, sit down—Jimmy makes excellent coffee," Brigitte said, her tone distracted. She herself perched on a chair by the coffee service, as if aware, in a corner of her mind, that no one would sit until *she* did.

"Sugar, cream?" she asked, filling two cups.

They both demurred.

"Then it's true," she said, a twinkle in her eyes. "Cops drink their coffee black."

"Not all of them," Mark assured her.

She looked over at her brother and then at the two detectives. "My cousin Charlaine is our family historian, and she lives here, but she's not in right now."

Mark produced a card from his pocket and handed it to Brigitte. "Would you ask your cousin to call us when she can, please?"

"Of course. I'm sorry—but I knew nothing about any of this."

"I hate to say it, but bad news is so common these days—I didn't even realize that two young women had recently been found dead," Alan Hildegard said. "But if you need our help in any way, you only need to ask."

They were being dismissed, Mark realized. Alan Hildegard had spoken, and that was the end of things.

Mark rose again. "Thanks for the coffee, and for your time."

"Yes, thank you," Brodie said.

The two of them left and were soon back in the car. When they drove toward the gate to leave, it opened automatically. Either that, or someone was watching and was anxious to see them leave.

"What do you think?" Brodie asked.

"I think they're shapeshifters," Mark said.

Brodie grinned. "Don't go doing Other profiling, now."

Mark grinned at that. "No, I mean that, as shape-shifters, they can give pretty much any impression they choose."

"Alan seemed sincerely upset by the deaths and the connection to the family."

"As did his sister."

"Let's hope the cousin contacts us soon," Brodie said. "For now, I don't know about you, but I have to get some sleep."

Mark glanced at him. "I'd like to go back to the House of the Rising Sun with you. I want to hear more about Alessande being a Keeper now."

"Sure. You can have the car if you want to go home afterward—or you can stay over at Pandora's Box. Rhiannon has a nice guest bedroom."

"Maybe I will crash there."

Brodie had a remote in his car and opened the large gate at the Keepers' estate. Wizard, Rhiannon's massive wolfhound mix, followed as they headed up the drive and parked.

The minute they stepped out of the car, Wizard barked happily, seeing friends. "Don't jump!" Brodie said.

But Wizard was already up, his giant paws on Brodie's shoulders.

"We're not doing so well with the dog training," Brodie said.

Mark grinned. "He's a good dog."

As if aware of the compliment, Wizard came running over to greet him.

Mark was prepared for the dog's embrace and the sloppy kiss on the cheek he received.

"Sorry—he's kind of slobbery," Brody said.

"He's fine," Mark said, wiping his face.

Brodie headed toward Castle House, where the others were still gathered. Mark started to follow him but was stopped by a loud "Psst!"

He paused, looking around. There was no one in sight.

He heard a self-satisfied giggle. Frowning, he spun around. He still didn't see anyone.

Then a mourning dove came sweeping out of the nearest tree to land on the sidewalk before him.

The bird suddenly morphed right in front of him.

And there was Alessande, looking very proud of herself, tossing back a strand of white-blond hair and staring at him with defiance.

"I can't believe I never knew about this! Shifting is amazing!" she said. "I'm well on the road to joining the ranks of the Keepers." Despite her ongoing impudent look, she spoke with gentle amusement. "Mark, please don't be offended, but I hope you know that now no one can tell me to stay out of any situation where shape-shifting is involved."

Chapter 4

It was wonderful. Incredible. Exhilarating.

Once she concentrated, shifting was easy—far easier than teleporting. Teleporting meant moving through time and space, while changing simply meant switching appearance.

Admittedly, she was on a bit of a high, and she hadn't been able to refrain from taunting Mark Valiente.

His expression wasn't pleasant as he looked at her, shaking his head. "It's all a big game to you, isn't it?"

"What?" she asked him.

"Stretch your muscles, test your power. Play bird and fly around the yard. Women are dead, Alessande, and you just want to prove that you're tougher and stronger and more talented than anyone else."

She didn't understand why his disapproval hurt so much.

Unless there was a grain of truth in what he was saying.

"No," she said, speaking softly, seeking dignity. "I'm trying to learn. You were born a vampire. You grew up nurtured, learning to live in a world where once you would have been seen as nothing more than a bloodthirsty monster. When it came to being Elven, I, too, was taught everything I needed to know. But shifting… This is new to me. No one knows what they can and can't do until they stretch their muscles, and I'm just trying to test mine. I'm not trying to be bigger or tougher or stronger. I just need to be involved—to help."

"You need to stay out of this," he said, and his tone seemed a shade gentler.

"Could *you* stay out of it?"

"I'm a cop."

"Why are you a cop? Because you have to be involved. You feel that people need you—and that's why you do what you do. Unless, of course, *you* feel a need to exercise *your* power."

He looked back at her, studied her, and she was dismayed to realize that he very clearly didn't like what he saw.

Why? Why did that bother her? She winced inwardly; she'd gotten into this because she knew what she had to do. She had to save Regina. And not just

Regina. More women would die if this conspiracy of occult terror wasn't stopped. And Mark…

Might have saved her life, despite her protestations to the contrary.

He turned to enter the house.

Maybe he had a right to look at her that way. Maybe things wouldn't have gone so well if he and Brodie hadn't shown up at the Hildegard mausoleum.

Startled and distraught by being so completely dismissed, Alessande stood at the door for a moment before reentering the house herself.

The Gryffald cousins were seated around the large table in the dining room. Declan Wainwright and Mick Townsend were with them. As Alessande entered, Brodie had just pulled up a chair and Mark Valiente was on his way to join them. She entered and saw that the table had become crowded. For a moment, she thought they weren't going to make room for her.

Brodie watched her hesitate, stood and grabbed one of the chairs standing by the wall, drawing it up and waiting for her to sit. The minute Alessande had claimed her chair, Barrie spoke up.

"Okay," she said. She had a pad and pencil because, despite having all the technology she could want, she was still a words-on-paper reporter at heart. "We have two dead women. Both were aspiring actresses—which may or may not mean anything, seeing as a high percentage of the young ladies who come to Hollywood are dreaming of being the next star on the Walk of Fame. But…" She paused, looking over at Mark. "Brodie called earlier and told us that when you went to the old Hildegard Studio, you found a new screenplay by Greg Swayze on one of the soundstages."

"I checked while you were gone," Rhiannon said. "They're going to be casting for the movie starting next week. It's a historical piece, set in New York in the Five Points area in the 1880s. The lead character is Jane Adams, the daughter of Irish immigrants who is trying to escape the poverty of the Five Points district. She becomes involved with a rich man and realizes he might be a serial killer."

"It's not being produced by Alan Hildegard, is it?" Mark asked sharply.

Rhiannon shook her head. "No. It's being produced by Blue Dove Entertainment. It was started by a couple college kids doing independent documentaries. That was fifteen years ago—they grew slowly but surely, and now they're at a point where they can compete with the big boys."

"We need to speak with Swayze and find out if he knew either of the murdered women. It's very possible that one of them had the copy of the screenplay we found," Mark said.

"Or that Regina did," Alessande said.

They all looked at her for a moment, silent.

"I realize it's been kept out of the media, but how were the two women killed?" she asked. "I know they were kept alive for a long time before their deaths, and the fear they must have lived with until the moment of…" She shuddered, then said, "But I don't know how they were actually killed."

"Their throats were slit," Mark said.

"Clean cuts," Brodie put it. "Mercifully, they would have died within seconds from blood loss."

"But they weren't *drained* of blood," Mark said.

"No," Brodie agreed.

"So," Sailor said, "they were kidnapped, held—and then, after an indeterminate amount of time, they were murdered, and their bodies were dumped."

"With any luck Regina is still alive," Mark said quickly, looking at Alessande. He offered her a hopeful smile.

Maybe he was feeling just a bit badly about the way he had treated her outside, she thought, and smiled at him in return.

"What did you think of Alan Hildegard?" Barrie asked. She'd been scribbling while the others were speaking.

"He seemed indignant that his family's vault had been desecrated," Brodie said.

"Did you believe him?" Alessande asked.

"I don't know," Mark said. "We met him and his sister Brigitte. They both said they had nothing to do with it and wanted the people who had been there charged, but…they're shapeshifters. Who knows what you're really seeing when you meet them."

Declan cleared his throat. "Shapeshifters aren't all monsters, you know."

"Of course not," Sailor said indignantly.

"But they *are* capable of putting up a front," Barrie said, looking at Declan.

"None of us should take offense," Alessande said. "Humans and Others are equally capable of tremendous goodness and tremendous evil."

"It's just that when Others are involved, the evil can be a lot more heinous than anything humans can manage," Mark said. "I think Brodie and I will have to start fresh in the morning. We need to get every scrap of information we can from the detectives who've been handling the women's cases."

"I want to go see Antony Brandt—the medical examiner—too," Brodie told them. "Luckily he was the M.E. on both cases."

"And he's a werewolf," Barrie said. "Thank God for small favors."

"For now, we should all get some sleep," Rhiannon said firmly.

"But she's out there—Regina is out there, somewhere," Alessande said. "We don't have much time left if we want to find her alive."

Sailor set a hand on Alessande's. "I know, but we can't go door to door looking for her. And everyone here is exhausted."

"But—"

"I think she's safe right now," Mark said. "Two nights ago in the cemetery…well, it was a fiasco, basically. It will take them several days to pull themselves back together. And we'll all be better with rest.

Especially you, Alessande. You've just discovered your mixed heritage, and you've been playing with your newfound talents. If we get ourselves killed, we'll be of no use to Regina, so we've really got to get some sleep."

Alessande nodded, accepting their wisdom. "All right."

"Tomorrow I'll take you to your house to get some of your own things," Mark told her. "But until we get to the bottom of this, you'll be safer here. We all need to stick together."

Mick grinned. "Well, Declan, Brodie and I have already been living on the grounds—and I don't think any of us plan on changing that."

"Nope, not me," Brodie said. "And like I told you, Mark, Rhiannon and I have a room for you."

"So, it's settled—let's sleep," Sailor said.

They all rose. "Hey," Brodie said. "Everyone remember to plug in your cell phones tonight. A dead battery will not be an acceptable excuse for falling out of contact."

Alessande spoke up. "Before we split up... Merlin and I had a conversation today. He thinks that maybe the someone who believes that Sebastian can come back to life is...Sebastian."

"Sebastian has been buried for years," Mark said.

"Yes," Alessande agreed. "But Merlin thinks he's hung around. And after all, if Merlin can stay here as a ghost, Sebastian's...*essence* could still exist, too, just waiting to be resurrected."

"There's a difference," Mark said a little harshly. "Merlin is a ghost. He doesn't have a solid form. Not everyone can see him. He doesn't exist *in the flesh*. Sebastian's essence may be out there somewhere, but that doesn't mean he can literally come back to life."

"He was an illusionist, and a shapeshifter, and he studied the occult," Alessande said. "We don't know what he might be capable of." She stared at them each in turn, hoping that at least one of them would acknowledge the validity of her words. When no one did, she quickly turned and left, heading back upstairs to her room.

Dr. Antony Brandt was a werewolf. He was also an excellent medical examiner, and the L.A. Other community was lucky to have him.

He was a senior M.E. and knew how to arrange things to get the cases he wanted to handle. He left the gang shootings and overdoses to his human co-workers and made sure to take care of any Others who came through the morgue.

He greeted Mark and Brodie in his office.

"Thank God your boss, that furry old coot of a friend of mine, put you two on this case. I'd given him a call, but it took that mess out at the Starry Night Cemetery to make him realize this had to be Other-related," Tony told them. "So far," he continued, "the victims have been human, but I understand that you suspect that the murderer—or murderers—has now kidnapped a young Elven woman."

"We're trying to find her before you're required to perform her autopsy," Mark said.

"Of course," Brandt said solemnly. "So, before we go in and I show you the bodies, let me tell you what I've learned. Both women were young and in perfect health. They kept themselves toned—ready for whatever a role demanded. It's a shame—a damned shame."

"Both were blonde and blue-eyed, yes?" Mark asked.

"Like Elven women?" Brandt asked shrewdly.

Mark and Brodie both nodded.

"Yes," Brandt said.

Mark leaned forward. "Were they starved? Did it appear that they were abused in any way? They both disappeared weeks before they turned up dead, and they had only died a short time before their bodies were discovered."

"No, as I said, they were both in excellent shape. They were not starved, they were not bruised. They showed no signs of being tortured before they were killed by a sharp, sure slice across the neck. They exsanguinated quickly, with loss of blood being the official cause of death."

"But there was no sign of any vampire attack?" Mark asked.

Brandt studied him. "If they were killed by a vampire or vampires, they were not killed for their blood. No one so much as sipped from them. I know how to find the marks, and neither woman had them." He sighed. "Though I'm always worried about vampire involvement when exsanguination is the presumed cause of death, and that's why I insisted on taking both cases."

"Any signs that either woman fought back?" Brodie asked.

Brandt shook his head. "No sign of defensive wounds whatsoever. But—and this is very important—they both had Transymil in their blood. Of course, the lab doesn't really know what they found. They believe the women were given something opium-based."

Mark and Brodie looked at one another. Transymil was a potion familiar to many in the Other community, but its use wasn't sanctioned. It was a sedative and hallucinogenic that had originated in the Transylvania region of Romania, and the plant that formed its base was difficult to grow in the United States. Conditions had to be perfect for it to survive, and even then, the drug was made from the flower, and the plant only flowered for a single week in the spring. Not that timing meant that much; once the drug was transformed into a liquid, it could retain its potency for years. Older Others frowned on its use and fretted over the younger generation using it much as human parents worried about their children becoming hooked on heroin.

"The lab technicians are reporting they don't know what they found?" Mark asked.

"I told you—they believe it to be opium-based,"

Brandt said. "And, really, does it make much difference? They think it's been chemically altered—just as half the drugs on the street are chemically altered. God only knows what street drugs contain these days."

True and, sadly, good for the Other community. Transymil's existence would not be discovered.

And bad. Very bad. Because Others with a mind to perpetrate evil could carry it off more easily than humans—especially when humans couldn't even pinpoint the cause.

"Alessande was drugged when we found her," Brodie said. "She said that she inhaled it, that it was in or on the bag that was thrown over her head."

"I'm guessing that's how the killer keeps his victims under control until he's ready to kill them," Mark said.

Brandt stood. "Enough talking. Let's do this."

The morgue was huge, which made sense given the population of L.A. alone dictated that it be so.

They went into a room filled with drawers and shelves and gurneys. There was never enough space for the dead. Some came in and were simply shelved, as if they were condiments in a grocery store.

But Leesa Adair and Judith Belgrave were in the drawers, and Brandt led them first to Leesa's body. He pulled the lever, opened the door, slid her out, and Mark was immediately filled with pity. There was something heartbreaking about the body minus the soul.

She had been beautiful as well as young. The world should have been hers to conquer. Even death couldn't hide the fact that she'd been filled with hope and humor. Something about her face still hinted at a quick and easy smile. The signature Y-shape of an autopsy incision split perfect skin.

"Lividity is on the back," Brandt said. "They were both killed lying down, then moved to the dump sites."

Next they examined the earthly remains of Judith Belgrave. Like Leesa, she had been tall and blonde and beautiful. Leesa had possessed a fuller face. Judith, even in death, had classic features and gave an impression of elegance, while Leesa could easily have portrayed the girl-next-door in any film.

Judith was very much like Alessande, Mark noticed with a shiver of unease.

"Any questions I can answer for you?" Brandt asked them.

Mark slowly shook his head.

Alessande was right; they had to find Regina—before Brandt was forced to open a third drawer to show them another victim.

"If you think of anything else—that drug would have been good to know about—please notify us immediately," Brodie said, his tone critical.

The fact that the victims so closely resembled his own race had to be unnerving for Brodie, Mark realized.

"And just how was I supposed to put that in the

report?" Brandt demanded. "I had a call in to the station, but even then, I have to be careful."

"Of course," Mark said quickly, to smooth the waters.

"I do my part here, but the Others on the force have to do *their* parts, too," Brandt said. "So you'll inform me if something comes up that I should know?"

"Of course," Mark assured him.

A few minutes later he and Brodie were back out in the California sun. Mark was glad. No matter how well it might be maintained, the morgue always smelled of chemicals on top of death.

"Transymil," Brodie said. "That's not good. Not good at all."

"It almost certainly means that someone local is manufacturing it, which is bad enough, but now that our cultists have gotten their hands on it…"

"You don't think the members themselves are the ones manufacturing it?"

Mark thought for a minute. "No, actually, I don't. I think the head of the cult and his followers are here in L.A. You've got to be up in the mountains to cultivate the plant, and you need privacy to transform it into liquid."

"True," Brodie agreed. "So, let's hit the streets. We'll find some junkies and see what they know."

"I have some friends in Vice—I can give them a call," Mark suggested.

* * *

Alessande walked aimlessly around the eclectic living room of Castle House. She knew that everyone was hovering to see to her safety, and it made her feel restless.

She paused, looking at Sailor. "I think Regina intended to audition for *Death in the Bowery* and that she was the one who left the screenplay there—right before she was taken." She resumed her pacing. "And I think I need to audition for that role."

Declan shook his head. "You might be recognized."

"Okay, aside from you taking that risk, you think she spent the evening at the House of Illusion, bought gas—and decided to break into the old Hildegard Studio to read a screenplay?" Sailor asked incredulously.

"No," Alessande said. "I think she met someone at the House of Illusion—someone who gave her the screenplay and sent her to the Hildegard Studio."

"Why send her to an empty studio?" Barrie asked.

"Maybe they said they'd meet her there. Maybe they suggested that she could practice there in secret."

"And maybe," Rhiannon said, "some other person with nothing to do with any of this left the screenplay there."

"Both options seem a little far-fetched to me," Declan said thoughtfully.

Rhiannon let out a deep sigh of frustration. "I

have to go—I'm playing at the Mystic Café this afternoon."

"That's not a bad thing," Mick told her, and offered her a smile of encouragement. "The local Others know it's owned by the Keeper of the canyon werewolves, so a lot of them feel comfortable there."

"And, at the moment—given what went on at the Hildegard tomb the other night—we need to look at all the Other races, including werewolves," Declan pointed out.

"I'll keep my eyes open and see what I can discover," Rhiannon said. She hesitated. "I also got asked to play tonight at the House of Illusion.

"Jerry feels bad about the killings and their connection to the House of Illusion," Rhiannon said. "I'm sure we can go to him for help, see if he remembers Regina or the dead women."

Alessande knew Jerry Oglethorpe, the owner, and the rest of the L.A. Otherworld were rocked by the recent spate of murders.

"So that's where we'll begin tonight," Sailor said, looking at Alessande.

Alessande smiled. "All right. I'll get online and find out where the auditions will be held."

"Well, since I'm really an actress, not a waitress," Sailor said, catching Declan's gaze and continuing, "I'll audition, too."

As Rhiannon had told them earlier, the auditions were next week, but every minute that went by, Alessande feared Regina was in greater danger. "I'll let you know about dates and times," she said.

"I doubt if they're going to hold open auditions for the main roles," Sailor said. "I have an easier way. I'll call my agent."

"On the street, we've been calling it XF. It's one hell of a scary drug and it's showing up in more and more places," Janet Scaly, an undercover cop in Vice, told Mark and Brodie as they gathered around her desk in an isolated corner of the precinct. She was a little pixie of a thing—literally. She really *was* a pixie. Barely five feet, with bright blue eyes and dark hair, she had a gamine's face, which made her perfect for Vice. Her size was deceptive, and she frequently worked undercover, because she looked like a runaway waif ready to play her guitar for money.

"Our chemists tell us that it's from a rare plant that originated in Eastern Europe, and it's still relatively new here, so a lot of Others don't know about it yet. Given where it originated, the vampires seem to be the ones growing it." She looked at Mark apologetically. "No insult intended, it's just, you know, it *is* from their part of the world. Anyway, that doesn't change the fact that we're trying to find the source and stop it."

"How is it being used on the street?" Mark asked.

"Date rape—it's the newest date rape drug," she said. "A few drops in your drink, and you're rendered anything from unconscious to unable to function, depending on your body weight. Pretty scary stuff—we had one junkie die. I think XF was the major factor, but it was hard to tell, there were so many drugs in her system. Sad. We're here in the city where dreams come true—but so do nightmares."

"Do you know who's selling the stuff?" Mark asked.

She gave him a long, dry look. "If I knew, don't you think they'd be under arrest?" She shrugged. "Hang out around the Hotel Clinton—it's a pay-by-the-hour. We found the latest dead junkie there in room 333."

"Thanks," Brodie told her. "Sounds like a little surveillance is in order."

They left Janet and the station, and headed down to the seedy area that hosted the Hotel Clinton. Brodie flashed his badge at the desk manager, who barely looked up as he nodded.

Mark sat in a chair and picked up a newspaper, and Brodie headed across to a worn-out sofa that faced an ancient TV.

They waited, and they watched.

"It's my understanding that you've already done some screen work," Lisa Morgan, a talent agent at the ITC Group, said to Alessande. "Who represented you?"

Alessande looked over at Sailor sitting next to her, thankful they could get in the very same day to see Sailor's agent and mentally crossed her fingers that the woman would take Alessande on. "I've only done extra work, actually. But when I heard there was an open call for this film, I had to give it a try," she told the woman.

Lisa Morgan was perfect for Hollywood. Her age was impossible to determine, but she had obviously had work done on her face—the telltale stretching was there. But it had been good work, and she cut an impressive figure. She wore a tight-fitting business suit, the skirt short but not too short, and four-inch heels, and her expertly dyed hair was swept up in a sleek chignon. Alessande made a point of catching her eyes to read her mind, hoping to learn something useful.

I'm not at all sure about this... The woman is really tall. And I don't know... They're friends, both wanting to read for the same role. Hmm. What the hell...maybe...

"All right. Let me see what you can do."

She reached into a drawer and took out a copy of the screenplay.

Death in the Bowery.

"You want me to read right here, right now?" Alessande asked.

"You want to be an actress, right? You'd better get used to cold readings," Lisa said flatly. "Let's go. Sailor, you be the villain—the rich banker, Martin Reilly. Alessande, you take Jane Adams, and then we'll switch it around. I want you to read from a scene toward the end of the screenplay. Jane is an orphan, poor but respectable, and she knows that Martin is a killer. She's trying not to let on that she knows, while he seduces her into going with him up to the room in the whorehouse that he owns—the room where he kills. Got it?"

Alessande nodded, and they began to read. Sailor easily took on the persona of the male villain, and Alessande found it easy to respond to her in character.

Halfway through the scene, Lisa had them switch parts, and once again Alessande was impressed by Sailor's talent.

When they were finished, they looked across the desk at Lisa, who nodded. "All right, I'll set up the auditions. I'll text you tomorrow with your times."

Alessande grinned as she and Sailor left the office. "I can't believe we're both in," she said.

Sailor laughed. "Yeah—you, me and a thousand hopefuls from around the world. But at least we'll get our chance to read."

"Will we meet the screenwriter there?"

"Most of the time, I'd say no. The writer is at the bottom of the totem pole—except that this one is Greg Swayze and he's the man of the moment. He might be there. But Brodie and Mark are cops. They can get in to see him."

"Cops don't necessarily get people to talk," Alessande said.

"No, but—"

"We need to get Brodie and Mark to stay away from him until we've had a chance to talk to him."

"We can try."

"Hey, you're the Elven Keeper. You can tell Brodie what to do."

"No, I can't. A Keeper can't tell someone not to do his job unless he's actively hurting someone. You need to realize that, now that you're going to be a Keeper."

"But, he'd listen to you," Alessande said. "Right?"

"I can try, but…"

"But?"

"Nothing."

"You were about to say that his partner is a vampire and doesn't have to pay any attention to you, weren't you?"

"The vampires do listen to Rhiannon," Sailor said, pride and loyalty in her voice.

Her phone began to ring. Sailor dug in her ample over-the-shoulder bag until she found it. She mostly listened, saying yes, and then no, followed by yes again.

"What's up?" Alessande asked when Sailor disconnected.

"We should head over to the House of Illusion. I need to get to work, and Rhiannon will be there soon. I think Barrie is going over with her, along with Declan and Mick. Brodie and Mark are on a case, but they'll meet us there later."

* * *

They'd been waiting for about an hour—a long hour in which Mark drove himself crazy thinking of other things he could be doing, wondering if this was all a waste of time—when a man finally entered with a girl of about eighteen on his arm.

And she really was resting virtually her entire weight on his arm, because she was barely standing. They were both tall, and the girl had long, white-blond hair.

"Hey, buddy, we need a room for a few hours. Just to have a rest, you know? My girlfriend here is wiped out," the man said, approaching the desk.

To Mark's dismay, the clerk looked nervously in his direction. "Minimum is fifty bucks for up to four hours," he said.

Luckily the man didn't seem to notice the clerk's nervousness; he just wanted to get the girl upstairs.

Mark rose and walked over to the desk. "Been sightseeing?" he asked.

The man looked at him and nodded. He was about twenty-five, wearing a sweatshirt with the L.A. Lakers logo. *Tourist my ass,* Mark thought.

"Big city, really big city, so much to see," the man said. His eyes were dilated. The girl's eyes weren't even open.

"Is your girlfriend all right?" Brodie asked, coming up on the man's other side.

Suddenly, the man shoved the girl at Brodie and turned to run.

Swearing, Mark looked at Brodie.
"I've got her—go!" Brodie said.
Mark took off running.

Chapter 5

Alessande had to admit that the House of Illusion was spectacular. With the exception of the coat check off to one side, the foyer felt like the entrance to a medieval fortress, and the room just beyond kept up the impression, resembling a king's great hall.

The impression was deliberate. The House of Illusion had been built in the 1890s specifically to resemble a medieval castle. There was a massive bar to the right of the great hall, and the numerous plank tables with bench seating could accommodate hordes of drinkers. Straight ahead was an open performance space that kept up the illusion of walking farther into the depths of a castle. The entrance to a small restaurant stood open just past the bar, while a hallway on the opposite wall led to the Magician's

Cave, a small venue where young magicians could practice their trade.

"There's a staging area in the basement, and trust me, it's creepy," Sailor said as they moved deeper into the club. "The three of us had just started out as Keepers when a few vicious rebels decided to challenge the old order, and they nearly succeeded. But that's all in the past," she finished cheerfully.

Alessande smiled, fascinated. She'd been here once in the early days, because the Others could be just as fascinated by illusion and magic as any human. And the House of Illusion was as magical as any real castle. Even she couldn't help but feel a bit awed by being here.

A tall man with white hair and a dignified demeanor was politely greeting people as they entered the great hall. When he saw them, his eyes lit up. "Sailor Gryffald! And who have we here? No, don't tell me." He lowered his voice. "You're Alessande Salisbrooke, correct?"

"Come on, Jerry," Sailor said, grinning. "That wasn't much of a feat of mind reading—you knew that we were coming."

"Guilty as charged. But, Alessande, I do remember you from years and years ago. Thankfully, you're an Elven and I'm a vampire, so all those years don't matter much, do they?" he teased.

"Is Rhiannon here?" Sailor asked, forestalling any discussion of the old days in favor of making progress on solving the problem at hand.

"Yes, and are you working tonight, as well? Or are you only here to see the show?"

Sailor laughed. "I'm just here to see the show, though I suppose I should have asked Barrie if I could afford a night off—she's our queen of household finance."

Jerry waved a hand in the air. "The old days were so much easier. If I was hungry, I fed upon an unwary traveler—oh, don't look so worried. I drank, but I never killed. And if I needed a place to stay, I hypnotized a nobleman and took over his house. These days, I pay bills just like everyone else. Come on. Rhiannon is doing an early set in the bar, and then she'll be free to sit with you. She has a late-night gig at the Snake Pit, so I assume you'll all be heading that way later."

Alessande wasn't all that fond of the Snake Pit—it was mainly an after-hours place for Others to hang out without worrying about letting their true nature slip, and she hadn't been particularly social for many years. She attended all the Elven councils, of course, but only because she didn't feel she really had a choice. She had been there when Sailor, as a newly minted Elven Keeper, had faced and defeated the Celebrity Virus, but her involvement had been accidental rather than intentional.

For so long she'd been happy in the background, using her skill with potions to help her fellow Others—and even humans—live happier and healthier lives. Staying in her own little world had been easy.

"There's Barrie," Sailor said. "We should go join her."

Just then they heard a smattering of applause. Alessande looked over to see that Rhiannon had entered the room wearing a medieval gown. It suited her. She carried her guitar and took up a position on the bar's small stage. Alessande saw Declan and Mick join Barrie at the table, talking casually to each other, but she didn't think for a minute that they were as nonchalant as they appeared.

"Welcome to the House of Illusion," Rhiannon said. "The real show will begin soon, but in the meantime…"

She began to sing as Alessande followed Sailor to join Barrie and the others.

"We've seen him. He's here," Barrie said excitedly as soon as they were seated.

"Who?" Alessande asked.

"Greg Swayze! The man who wrote *Death in the Bowery.*"

Mark was getting tired of chasing down suspected criminals. Why couldn't they just stop and wait like civilized human beings once it was clear there was no escape? He could, of course, call on his vampire speed, but that would attract attention. Even so, he might have to resort to that, because this perp could run like a son of a gun.

The human had knocked over trash cans and newspaper stands and anything he could find along the way, forcing Mark to hop, veer and twist in an effort to catch up.

Screw it.

He went into vamp mode and stopped ten feet in front of his suspect. The man saw him, and his eyes widened, but he was too close to stop and slammed straight into Mark. With considerable effort, Mark kept them both upright, and he instantly spun the man around and cuffed him.

"Hey!" his prisoner protested. "You can't do this! Am I under arrest? You haven't read me my rights."

"I *can* do this—for resisting arrest if nothing else."

"But—"

Mark sighed and read the man his rights, then informed him that he was under arrest for battery.

"Battery? I didn't hurt anyone. I mean yeah, we were arguing, but just normal boyfriend-girlfriend stuff. I—"

"That young woman you were with is half dead, thanks to whatever drug you gave her."

"Hey, I didn't make her take anything."

"We'll have to ask *her* that, won't we?"

"You have to prove—"

"I don't have to prove anything until you're arraigned," Mark said. "Let's go. I'd like to get back to the fine hotel where you were taking the lady to 'rest.'"

The guy's shoulders slumped as all the fight went out of him, and he went peacefully.

At the hotel, Mark found that an ambulance had already arrived and the young woman was on her way to the hospital. And Brodie briefed Mark on the rest to bring him current on this case. Brodie had called in the situation to Lieutenant Edwards next.

Then the girl had roused long enough to tell Brodie that her name was Chelsea Rose. She was a local, a hostess at an upscale restaurant in Beverly Hills and an acting hopeful. Thereafter she had lapsed back into unconsciousness and he'd called her parents, who would be meeting her at the hospital.

The prisoner was Terry Steiner; by the time they had him in the car to bring him to the station, he was talking a blue streak.

"Look, I just heard about this stuff—they said it was better than Ecstasy. You find a girl, and she's yours. I'm crazy about Chelsea—I'd never hurt her. I've used every cent I've made to go to that lousy high-priced rip-off joint where she works just to see her. I talked her into an adventure today once she was done with her shift. We bought the stuff—hell, neither one of us knew it was going to knock her out!"

"Where did you get it?" Mark demanded. The kid was no Other; he had no special powers. His story rang true. "And where did you hear about it?"

"Man, everyone's heard about it," Steiner said. "But finding someone who knows where to get it… I was at a club, and I heard some guys next to me saying you could buy it on the street."

"On the street where?" Brodie asked.

He gave them the address. Mark and Brodie looked at one another.

Terry Steiner had bought the drug just around the corner from the Snake Pit.

"How can we manage to talk to him?" Barrie asked thoughtfully.

Alessande smiled. Barrie was an investigative reporter, one of the best in the city. But because she was such a good reporter, she overthought things at times. "I know how," she said. "Where is he?"

"To the left of the stage, and he's totally into Rhiannon."

Alessande looked in the direction Barrie had pointed out.

Greg Swayze appeared to be somewhere in his late thirties or early forties. His hair was dark, cut short, with a lock that fell over his forehead. He was seated, so she couldn't judge his height, but he had a medium build and looked very fit.

"It's easy," Alessande said, smiling. "Watch and learn." She made her way between tables until she reached his. There was room next to him on the bench, so she sat down. He was so entranced by Rhiannon that he didn't even notice her at first, so she tried to get a feel for him.

He wasn't, she determined, any kind of Other. He was human.

At last he turned her way. "Well. Hello."

"Hi," Alessande said.

He smiled, and she called on her Elven talents, willing herself to be as seductive as possible. His smiled turned to a slight frown, and she wondered if he knew there were such things as Elven. Or maybe he just sensed something different about her.

She quickly read his mind. She didn't get much.

I'd like to get this one in bed! Legs that stretch forever. And in damned good shape.

"You're Greg Swayze," she said.

He seemed startled that she knew, and he blinked and looked at her chest instead of her eyes. That was a problem for any woman of course, but especially so for Elven women. "Do I know you?"

"We've never met, no. But of course I know who *you* are."

"You do? That's interesting. Most people know actors and actresses. Actors and actresses know the top agents and producers and directors—and even casting agents. I'm just a writer. The bottom rung of the ladder. No one knows *me*."

She smiled. "That's not true. You're not just any writer. You write a screenplay, and you hang on to it. You stick with the project. No one rewrites you a thousand times just so a new name can go on the credits. Producers and directors, not to mention actors and actresses, trust you."

He laughed at that. "I had one success. One tremendous success, I admit. And that's because I made a cheap movie that more or less went viral and made a fortune."

"I *loved* it," Alessande lied. She'd never even seen the thing.

"Ah! You're an actress. I should have realized it, given the way you look. Obviously you want a part in my new film. Well, don't worry. If they don't cast you, call me and I'll get you in somewhere. I'll bet the camera loves you. What have you done?"

"Not much," she admitted. "But I *am* going in to audition tomorrow. I'm waiting for my time. Will you be there?"

"I wasn't planning on it," he admitted. "But now... you can count on it."

She smiled sweetly at him. "I'll be coming with a friend," she said.

"Oh?"

She pointed out Sailor.

"Very pretty girl," he said. He looked back at Alessande. "But there's only one lead role."

"But there are...victims, right?" Alessande asked.

He nodded. "Can I buy you a drink?" He leaned closer. For a moment, she read his thoughts again.

Oh, man, this is cool. Most actresses know writers don't have much power, so they ignore us. But this one... She's hot and blonde and tall, and I could get lucky tonight.

Alessande stood quickly. "I would love to, but I'm here with friends, and I don't... Well, when I make a date, even with friends, I keep it. Wonderful to meet you, Mr. Swayze. Your work is really remarkable."

He looked up at her, and she caught his eyes and read his mind for a minute.

She's stunning, and so bright. I have to have her....

She turned away quickly. She'd done everything she'd needed to do.

As she returned to her table, Declan started to move to make room for her. She quickly shook her head.

It was important that she not appear to be attached to either of the men in any way. She looked meaningfully at Barrie, who quickly slid over to give her room.

But just as she sat down, someone slipped in next to her.

She turned to see who it was, and dismay filled her as she realized that Mark Valiente had just joined her.

"Don't sit there, please!" she said quickly.

"Look, I know you have a thing against vampires—"

"I like vampires just fine. It's just—"

"Just that you have something against me?"

"No! Please. I'm working on getting a role in *Death in the Bowery.*"

He sighed, looking down. "Listen, Alessande, that screenplay may have nothing to do with this."

"Or it may have *everything* to do with it."

He winced, gritting his teeth. "Is that the guy— the screenwriter—over there?"

"Yes."

"All right, give me the brush-off," he said.

He turned to look at her as if he had just discovered her, a lone woman, sitting where a man could hit on her.

"Um, leave, please?" she asked.

He smiled slightly, and he was suddenly absolutely charming. "You don't give a brush-off very well."

She stood, staring down at him. "Get the hell away from me," she said.

It was perfect. Her voice carried. People turned.

"Fine. Have a nice night!" Mark said, standing. Then he added softly, "I won't be far. We have to head to the Snake Pit soon."

Alessande didn't acknowledge his words as she sat again and turned to the other women. "He said he'd see us at the Snake Pit as soon as Rhiannon finishes."

"Swayze keeps watching you," Barrie said.

"He seemed pleased when you blew off Mark," Sailor commented.

"Let's hope he's watching both of us," Alessande said.

"If he gets a say in casting the leading lady, the part is yours."

Alessande smiled. "Yes, but if the movie's legit and the screenplay had nothing to do with the kidnappings, you're the real actress. It would be a great role for you."

"I'm a Keeper first," Sailor said.

"But even Keepers are allowed to dream and have real lives," Alessande said.

There was a burst of applause as Rhiannon finished her set and announced that they were all invited to move into the next room and watch the magic show.

Alessande felt a hand on her shoulder. It was Brodie.

"Luckily we only have three cars here, so no one will be alone. You're with Mark and me."

"But—"

"Swayze just went into the show. He won't see anything."

Barrie took her arm, urging her toward the door. "Let's move fast, just for safety."

When Alessande was seated in the back of Brodie's car—she'd insisted on the backseat; she was tall, but Mark and Brodie were taller—she leaned back, tired and confused. "I'm not sure why we didn't stay to watch the show. Tonight's magician is a shifter. And I can tell you this, shapeshifters are involved."

"We need to find out what's going on at the Snake Pit," Mark said.

"Then ask Declan Wainwright. He owns the place!" Alessande snapped.

"I managed to speak with Declan when we arrived," Brodie said. "He knows we're on the hunt."

"What *is* going on at the Snake Pit? I can't believe that Declan—"

"No, but I believe someone who hangs out at the Snake Pit *is* involved. They're selling a drug called XF, real name Transymil, on the streets," Mark explained.

"There's a girl still in the hospital who took some earlier today," Brodie said.

"And a kid in jail swearing that he thought they were just doing some new form of Ecstasy," Mark said.

"I can't believe they're selling it on the streets now." Alessande felt cold. The idea of it becoming widely disseminated was really scary.

"Alessande," Brodie said slowly. "Can you...can you do anything about that?"

"About what?" she asked.

"The poor girl remains unconscious. The hospital is struggling, because they haven't got the chemical breakdown of the drug, so they don't know how to counter it. Could you come up with an antidote?"

"I...I don't know. I've never tried to make one. Transymil's always been kept among Others, and they usually make it back all right from a trip," she said.

"But you could try, right?" Mark asked.

She nodded. "I'd have to get to my house, though."

"Tomorrow," Brodie said.

"I have an audition tomorrow," she said. Mark

was staring at her. "We have to follow the screen-play. I know it's important. I can feel it in my gut."

"Right after the audition," Mark said firmly.

"All right," she agreed.

They drove up to the sweeping entrance of the Snake Pit. A tall, striking leprechaun named Barney came right over to the car, but he was more than a valet, Alessande knew. He was Declan's eyes and ears, as well.

"Declan just went in. He got here ahead of you, with Sailor and Rhiannon Gryffald," the leprechaun said.

"Thanks, Barney." Brodie tossed him the keys. "Can you keep the car where—"

"You have easy access," Barney said gravely. "Yes, I'll put you at the end of the row."

"Great. I have keyless entry, so just throw the keys under the passenger's seat, will you?"

Barney nodded. They exited the car and headed for the door, where Mark abruptly turned away. "I'll take the street," he told Brodie.

"I'll get Rhiannon and keep her with me. Whoever's selling the stuff, he's going after men who have women with them."

Mark looked at Alessande skeptically. "She can come with me."

"I'm not *she*. You know my name," Alessande said.

"Sorry," Mark said, clearly aggravated. "*She* is better than *that vampire cop,* though."

Brodie laughed suddenly. "You two go on. Anyone watching will definitely think you need help if you're trying to get into bed with Alessande."

"Let's head out, shall we?" Alessande asked. She started down the sidewalk without waiting to see if Mark was following her.

A moment later she felt his hand on her shoulder and turned around. He dusted her off, as if there had been something there.

"What was *that* for?" she asked him.

"Just trying to knock off the chip," he said.

"Shall I return the favor?"

He didn't reply, only walked silently at her side.

There was so much tension between them, she wanted to apologize; she didn't know why he made her so defensive all the time. This was probably her fault. He'd thought he'd saved her life, and he saw that as his job, because he was a cop. But she... She had been hostile, because he seemed to think that she was...

Incompetent.

She stopped and turned and looked at him. She managed a smile. "I guess I'd better at least walk with you. I have to make it look like there's some hope, right?"

He grinned and slid an arm around her shoulders. The warmth, the weight of it, felt good.

"We're turning the corner, and once we do...we'll be in a far shadier part of the city."

"Los Angeles is that way, isn't it?" Alessande said.

"Multimillion-dollar mansions just down the block from crack houses."

He nodded. "The dream—and then the fulfillment of the dream. Or not."

It was so true. The Snake Pit was splendor personified, but now, right around the corner, they saw those who spent their hours on doorsteps and leaning against buildings. Some had cigarettes they barely managed to smoke; some were drinking alcohol out of containers hidden by brown paper bags.

There were a few lit storefronts, and people who were making a legitimate living at something were buying groceries, their children holding tightly to their hands.

"Down one more street—and then we need to argue about where we are," Mark said.

"Okay," Alessande agreed.

They turned the corner; the road sloped downward, echoing the trend in the lives of those who lived there.

"Oh, this is ridiculous!" Alessande said, pulling away from his hold. "You don't have the faintest idea where we are. We're lost!"

"I am *not* lost," Mark protested. "I'm just getting my bearings."

"Well, get them quickly. You promised me dinner—a *good* dinner—and then a movie. Not a walk down a dark and…" She paused to look around and lowered her voice. "A dark and dangerous street."

"Hey, you two need some help?"

She spun around. A man was approaching them from the rear. He was in jeans and a T-shirt that advertised a heavy-metal band. He looked fairly decent, except that his jeans hadn't seen the inside of a washer for a long time. Alessande tried to catch his eyes as he approached them.

Perfect targets.

That was all she got, and then he looked at Mark.

Mark towered above the man. "We're fine," he said sharply.

"We're lost," Alessande said at the same time.

"Well, not to worry. I can get you back to Sunset, and you should be fine after that," the man said. "But…"

"But what?" Mark asked him.

"But…how did you manage to get yourselves here anyway? This area isn't safe—not for someone who looks like her."

Alessande made a move toward Mark, who put his arm around her protectively.

"Sweet. You two *are* a couple, right?" the man asked.

"Who are you?" Mark asked sharply.

"They call me Digger around here. I'm always digging for a way to make a living, you know?"

"Um, nice to meet you, Digger," Alessande said.

"The pleasure is mine. So what were you doing in this area anyway? Were you by any chance looking for someone?" Digger said. "Or some*thing?*"

"There's a guy who was supposed to set me up," Mark admitted.

"Yeah, I figured. Well, who?"

"I don't know. He called himself Chameleon," Mark said.

"I don't know this Chameleon, but maybe I could set you up."

"What have you got?" Mark asked.

"Honey…" Alessande said nervously.

"Don't worry," Digger said. "I promise you, I'll give you good stuff. I make my living on return customers."

"He could be a cop," Alessande whispered to Mark, but loud enough for Digger to hear.

"Lady, do I look like a cop?" Digger demanded.

"No, and that's why you could be one."

"What do you have?" Mark asked.

"All the usual stuff…"

"We don't want the usual," Mark said. "We're looking for something different."

"Well, I got a little pill I guarantee you've never had before." Digger inclined his head toward Alessande, giving Mark a conspiratorial wink. "It could melt the polar ice caps."

"I'll take two," Mark said.

"You just need one, but it never hurts to be ready for next time. And when you find out that you've gotten the next best thing to heaven, you know where to find me."

"Where do you get these from anyway?" Mark asked.

"Oh, no, buddy. You don't get my source."

"All right, that's fair," Mark said.

Digger quoted a price, Mark came up with the money, and Digger gave him the pills. "Excuse me, folks. I'll be leaving now, just in case cops are hanging out around here. Have fun!"

He took off down the street, then turned to watch them from behind the corner of a building.

Mark pulled her close and pretended to slip a pill into her mouth.

But the feel of his fingers as he'd looked into her eyes had been hypnotizing....

Of course. He's a vampire. Vampires use their eyes to...

The brush of his fingers was followed by that of his lips. She was startled; she hadn't expected him to take things so far.

And then there was the feel of his lips. A pressure that was confident and seductive, tinged with the sweetness of liquid fire....

She returned the kiss, accepting the warmth of his mouth, the sweep of his tongue. A heat seemed to grow in her, and she moved her fingers deftly through his hair.

They were acting, of course. This was Hollywood. Everything was an act.

And yet...

And yet she knew that she was really and truly—

and possibly dangerously—attracted to him. She hadn't let herself become involved with anyone in forever, but now she didn't want to end the kiss or lose the feel of him, the pressure of his body, the strength of his hands…ever.

His mouth lifted just an inch from hers. "All right, we're good. We need to walk back toward the Snake Pit, convince him we're gone."

"And then?" she asked. She looked into his eyes, which were a beautiful shade of gold, and then at his lips, which still seemed to whisper against her mouth and render her limbs weak and…

And hungry.

"Then we let him go tonight. We analyze the pill. You create the antidote."

He still held her. He hadn't moved. His fingers slowly caressed her cheek.

Acting.

"But Digger will get away. We won't get to his source."

"Digger has to trust us," he whispered. "Then we'll be able to find his source."

"Regina is still out there."

"I know—but we have to be patient and get the information we need."

"They could kill her anytime. She could be—"

"She's not dead. We *will* find her," he vowed. "Now lean against me. Pretend you're growing weak."

That was easy enough to do. She stumbled, and not on purpose.

"Perfect," he said softly.

And it was. She leaned against him and suddenly began to wonder about the heat that radiated from him.

He was a vampire....

He should be cold.

Instead he burned with a fire that could all too easily consume her.

Chapter 6

The Snake Pit was hopping. By the time Mark and Alessande returned, the others had taken a booth upstairs in the elegant room where snowy-white linen dressed the tables, the food was superbly prepared and the drinks were served in crystal.

Rhiannon was already on stage, singing a soft ballad. She acknowledged them with a nod as they entered.

Mark had his hand on Alessande's back as they neared the booth. It was the kind of polite gesture any man might offer, and she seemed to take it as such. Her calm amazed him. He still felt as if he were twitching inside. Apparently their kiss—which he had initiated just to see how far she was willing to go to play their dangerous game—had disturbed him far more than it had her.

Far more than he had ever expected.

The woman's an Elven, he told himself. *What did you think you would feel?*

Not this.

He'd known Elven all his life. They were exceptionally charismatic, the men handsome, the women beautiful. And Alessande was the epitome of Elven beauty: slender and fit, yet somehow voluptuous, as well. The feel of her in his arms was like a siren call.

That was it, nothing more. He'd thought to throw her off balance. Well, tables turned. He should have known!

His hostility toward her came from the moment when they had first met. She'd been angry, convinced she had had everything under control and that he'd ruined her grand plan.

On top of it all, he couldn't shake the strange daydream he'd experienced right before he had met her. If he closed his eyes now, he could still hear the music, see the beauty of the church arrayed for a wedding…see the river of blood that ran down the aisle.

He could still see the crystalline beauty of her eyes, could still feel her body pressed to his, as if she had left an indelible impression on his flesh.

"Well?" Brodie asked, breaking into Mark's thoughts.

"Success," Mark said, sliding into the rich velvet-upholstered booth next to Alessande. "Any news here?"

"Declan is working the crowd—easy for him to do, since he owns the place," Mick told him. Like Barrie, Mick was a reporter. He was great at ferreting out whatever was going on beneath the surface in a city that offered magic along with the normal underhanded deals, scandal—and murder.

Mark noticed that Barrie wasn't with them, but before he could ask about her absence, Alessande spoke up.

"Where's Barrie?"

"Interviewing Katrina Manville," Mick said.

"Why was she so interested in interviewing a costume designer *tonight?*" Alessande asked.

"Because she's doing costumes for *Death in the Bowery,*" Mick said.

"Oh!" Alessande said. "I didn't know."

"We didn't, either—until Declan said something just a moment ago," Sailor told them.

Alessande suddenly turned to him. She was close enough that her shoulder brushed his. "Let's dance," she said.

Mark looked at her with surprise. He felt a slight smile curve his lips. "You're asking me to dance?"

"I want to hear what Barrie's saying," she said. "And they're sitting right beside the dance floor."

Barrie would report anything she learned, he knew, but he couldn't resist the opportunity to hold Alessande in his arms.

Fool, he told himself.

He led her out to the dance floor. Rhiannon had been joined by a couple backup musicians, and they were playing something that he was pretty sure was a rumba. Luckily he had learned the steps years ago on a trip to Miami.

He danced Alessande over toward the two women. Thankfully, like most Others, his hearing was acute—and so was Alessande's. They didn't have to be right on top of Barrie to hear her conversation.

As they swept by, he noticed that Katrina was tall. Just not quite as tall as Alessande. Her hair was blond...though not quite the spun blond of Alessande's. And her eyes were blue, too. Though not quite the same clear blue-green of Alessande's, a color that could make a man think of endless days spent floating between the heavens and the seas....

Stop! he commanded himself. Honestly, he was going to make himself vomit if he didn't curtail his ridiculous mooning over her. He forced himself to listen to what Katrina was saying.

"They're re-creating 1880s New York and the Five Points district. The costuming will be late Victorian, and range from extremely elegant to the rags worn by those who were just scratching to stay alive. In those days... Well, you really couldn't blame a young woman coming from the gutters if she was willing to sleep her way up in society."

"How did you become involved in this particular project? Did you already know the screenwriter?"

"No, I only met Greg Swayze recently. I was hooked up by a friend."

"Who?"

Katrina sipped from a crystal champagne glass. "Brigitte Hildegard. Her brother's production company had considered bidding on it, but it was too pricey for them. She loved the screenplay, though, and thought it needed the best."

As they whirled away, Alessande looked at Mark with her eyes sizzling. "See?" she said.

"Barrie would have shared that information with us."

She ignored that and said, "I *knew* it. There's something going on with the movie!"

"Alessande," he murmured.

She looked at him with a question in her eyes.

He smiled. "I don't want you getting hurt," he said.

She actually smiled back at him. "I don't really want a role in it, you know."

"I didn't mean it that way."

He was startled when she rose up slightly on her toes to kiss his cheek. "Please, don't worry about me. I am Elven. And I'm destined to be a Keeper of shapeshifters—somewhere, sometime. Mick and Declan have both told me that my progress in dealing with my powers is amazing. I'm begging you, have some faith in me."

The music ended. For a moment they stood on the dance floor, just looking at one another. Then Declan came by and tapped him on the shoulder. "We're going to call it a night. The Hildegards don't seem to be coming out tonight and Barrie says she's gotten some interesting information about—"

"We know. We heard," Mark said.

"And tomorrow—" Declan began.

"There's a lot to do," Mark finished.

It still took them a few minutes to leave. Declan had to say his goodbyes to the staff and leave the place in the capable hands of his manager, a werewolf named Gregor.

But soon enough they were on their way out the door. And even then, Mark discovered, he couldn't keep his hands off Alessande. He touched her arm to guide her, the small of her back just to let her know he was there.

It was all right, he told himself. He was simply behaving the way any polite escort would.

Except, of course, any escort wouldn't be imagining the perfection of the woman as she lay naked, eyes alight, on a bed of silk, waiting for him....

He gave himself a shake.

And when they reached the House of the Rising Sun, he told himself that he was grateful when she went to Castle House, while he was a guest at Pandora's Box.

He told himself—but he didn't believe it.

* * *

She was dreaming again.

Except this time, the dream was erotic. So erotic that she could feel herself blush in her sleep.

And if a dream could have such a thing, it had *foreplay.*

She wasn't sure where she was. The room had a massive bed with blood red silk sheets. There were open doors that led to a balcony, and a breeze drifted in. Sheer white curtains fluttered in that breeze, and she felt the cooling air against the fire of her skin.

She lay there feeling the luxury of the silk. She was tense and aroused by simple anticipation. Because he would be with her any second.

And a second later...he was.

He came toward her out of the shadows. In the moonlight that bathed the room in a soft glow, he seemed as sleek and agile as a jungle cat. His chest was muscled steel. He was bronzed and beautiful.

He moved up on the foot of the bed and over her until the heat of his body blanketed her with vivid and electric force. She was achingly aware of the gold sizzle in his eyes, the contours of his face, the hard and masculine feel of him. Then his lips touched hers....

And she knew that kiss....

Except that this time it went deeper, then deeper still. His hands moved along her naked flesh and, wherever he touched her, it felt as if a star exploded. With every brush of his fingers becoming more in-

timate, she burned and writhed beneath him, and
touched him in turn....

"Alessande?"

She started and snapped up to a sitting position,
completely confused.

It was morning, she realized quickly, reluctantly
letting go of the dream.

She was at Castle House, with light pouring in
through the guest room window, and Sailor had just
tapped at the door, poked her head in and called
Alessande's name.

Alessande found herself praying that her arousal
hadn't been obvious—and that she wasn't naked, as
she'd been in the dream.

She was breathing heavily, and she felt a sheen of
sweat on her body, but, thank God, she was clothed.

"I'm sorry—we have to be up and out. Auditions
today."

"Of course," Alessande said. She made a pretense
of yawning, and smiled. "I'll hop in the shower and
be right down."

Sailor smiled and left her.

Alessande got up and headed for the bathroom.

Her shower was very, very cold.

Chelsea Rose was still in the hospital and quite
possibly dying.

The doctors reported that she had not regained
consciousness, and they feared that whatever she'd
been given might prove to be fatal.

Meanwhile, Terry Steiner remained in jail, await-ing arraignment. And Mark and Brodie were sitting in front of Bryce Edwards's desk and listened while he spoke with the district attorney's office. They were discussing what charges to file against Steiner. If the girl died, he might find himself facing murder charges, with manslaughter as the minimum.

Edwards hung up and looked at them. "Where are you two on this?"

Mark reported the events of the previous night.

"Why didn't you go after the source?" Edwards demanded.

"I needed to get Digger to trust me. Then he can lead me to the core of this thing," Mark explained.

"Bring him in—he'll crack," Edwards said harshly.

"On the plus side, I got the pills. The lab has them now. As soon as they come up with an analysis, Ales-sande can get started on an antidote."

"And where were you during all this?" Edwards asked Brodie.

"In the Snake Pit—chatting with every Other I could find," Brodie said.

"Did you discover anything?"

"I did find out that the Hildegard family comes in several nights a week," Brodie said.

"Great. An excuse for you two to spend your nights hanging at the Snake Pit," Edwards said.

"Barrie interviewed Katrina Manville," Brodie said.

Edwards arched a brow. "The costume designer? Because...?"

"She's associated with the screenplay we found at the old Hildegard Studio," Mark explained. "She's doing costumes for the show. She said Hildegard wanted to do the movie but passed due to budget concerns."

"So Hildegard isn't making the movie. That doesn't seem to get us anywhere," Edwards said.

"But it does," Brodie told him. "It means that Hildegard was very aware of the screenplay—he might even have started giving actresses copies of it before he decided to opt out of the bidding."

"We're going back to the Snake Pit tonight," Mark chimed in. "There's a connection here that passes right through the community of Others. The dead women followed a path that brought them to the House of Illusion and then right past—maybe into—the Hildegard Studio. The ceremony we broke up took place at the Hildegard tomb—in an old cemetery that was wholly owned by the Hildegard family at one time. Meanwhile, we've got an old Other-related drug suddenly being sold on the streets to anyone with the money to buy it," he went on. "So Brodie and Rhiannon are going over to the old studio again this afternoon to see if there's anything we've missed. Alessande and Sailor are reading for a role in *Death in the Bowery* right now, and Mick and Barrie are digging into the public records to find out who else is associated with the production."

"This could get dangerous," Edwards said, frowning. "And you're involving a number of civilians."

"Keepers," Brodie reminded him.

Edwards was silent for a minute, pursing his lips. Then he looked at them sternly. "Why are you in my office? Get out there and get this stopped!"

"He's in a great mood," Brodie noted as they left.

"Yeah—it's probably a good thing neither of us thought to remind him that he's the one who asked us to sit down and give him a report."

"He knows. He's just stressed," Brodie said.

"Yep. First, he's got a major problem on the streets, because that drug is deadly for humans. And then he's got two murdered women and knows we're in a race against time to save a third—and that somehow the Other community is involved." He paused, then went on. "Here's the thing. We've got a cult that believes they can bring back a dead shapeshifter magician via human sacrifice. And to keep their sacrificial victims silent, they're drugging them until they're ready for the kill. And because the dead women both had Transymil in their systems and it started showing up on the street at the same time the cult surfaced, I think there's got to be a connection. I'm inclined to change my earlier theory and my guess now is the cultists are manufacturing the drug and selling it on the side to make money. The timing is just too perfect for it to be a coincidence." He paused. "And I wouldn't be at all surprised if the Hildegards themselves are involved. Maybe we should be checking into the family finances."

"Let's start with the lab, see if they've got that analysis so Alessande will have something to work with," Brodie said. "And then we can stop by Forensic Accounting—see what they can find out without our having to get a warrant."

"What did you think of Alan Hildegard?" Mark asked.

"I think I'd like to know more about him. And his sister. And the cousin we have yet to meet."

"Let's hope they're at the Snake Pit tonight."

"I wonder how those auditions are going," Brodie said.

Mark was aching to know, as well. He was more worried than ever about Alessande's safety.

They had picked up the lab results and were on their way to Forensic Accounting when Mark's phone rang.

To his surprise, it was Alan Hildegard.

"Detective, my cousin is here. She's interested in meeting with you and answering whatever questions she's able to. When can you stop by?"

He glanced at his watch. Alessande and Sailor wouldn't be free for another two hours. Of course, in L.A., the drive to pick them up could take two hours.

He decided to trust in the great overlords of traffic and glanced at Brodie as he spoke into the phone. "Now, if that's good for you. Say…twenty minutes?"

"Perfect."

As he ended the call, Mark reflected that it sounded as if Hildegard had almost purred the word.

All Alessande had done before, when it came to acting, was arrive on set, where she was handed her costume and sometimes sent to makeup and hair, after which she followed the herd of extras to wherever they were told to go, followed by wait, wait and wait some more, punctuated by occasional bouts of doing some specified action, until the scene was shot to the director's liking. She had never been bitten by the acting bug and was always glad to get back home to the country, where she could take long walks in the woods, listening to the birds and the gurgling stream that crossed her property. Maybe she had been living a little on the antisocial side, but she'd been around a long time, and it was good to find peace at last.

The movie business, to her, was anything but.

Today's routine was at least different, though, because a real role was up for grabs. She waited in an outer office while Sailor went in to read. A few minutes later Sailor came out and gave her a thumbs-up, and Alessande took a deep breath and went in.

The room held a long table and, on the far side, four chairs, one of which was taken by Greg Swayze. He didn't speak to her, though he smiled. A man seated near the center of the row stood.

"Hello, I'm Taylor Haywood. I'm directing the film. This is Milly Caulfield to my right, casting di-

rector, and to her right, Tilda Lyons, associate producer. And Miss Gryffald told me you had a chance
to meet our screenwriter, Mr. Swayze, last night."
He nodded toward Greg, sitting to his left.

She smiled and said hello to the tribunal that
would decide her fate. The director was young—
she was afraid to think about how young—but she
had heard his name before, which was a good sign.
Milly Caulfield seemed to be old Hollywood; she
was skinny as a beanpole, dressed in stereotypi-
cal business attire, and her glasses were attached
to a delicate chain to keep her from losing them.
The associate producer, Tilda Lyons, was no spring
chicken, and she'd clearly had work done on her face,
but her plastic surgeon had been skillful.

"Excellent look—just right for the part." Alessande, grateful for her enhanced hearing, heard Tilda
whisper.

"Yes, but can she act?" Milly whispered back.
She was apparently not fond of the beautiful-but-dim
bombshell types who so often did so well.

Alessande didn't really care about the movie, of
course. She only wanted to find out why actresses
who had been reading the script had been disappearing. But she couldn't help it; Milly's implied insult
offended her.

Then it was time for her to read. Haywood handed
her the script, and they went straight to the pages
she'd read the day before, only this time he read the
villain's lines.

When she was done, he thanked her. She was expecting that to be followed by "Don't call us, we'll call you." But she didn't hear those words. Instead he said, "Miss Salisbrooke, let me ask you, would you be interested in any of the smaller parts in the film? There are a number, most with only a few lines but some with fairly meaty dialogue."

"Of course, thank you. I'm interested in working on the film in any capacity. I love the screenplay," she said, and smiled at Greg Swayze, who smiled back.

"That's wonderful. We'll be in touch. I'm sure you realize we're seeing many actors before we make our final decisions, so you may be asked for a callback."

"That will be fine, thank you."

She felt awkward. They weren't mean; they weren't cold. Still, she felt as if she were standing before a Roman tribunal or something equally daunting.

She thanked them again, then turned to the door.

Sailor was waiting for her in the outer office. "How did it go?" she asked.

"They asked me if I was interested in other parts," Alessande said. "Is that good?"

"Me, too. And it's certainly better than a flat turndown. Come on. Declan is waiting for us."

"I thought Mark and Brodie were going to pick us up?"

Sailor shook her head. "Mark called and said they were held up, so he wants us to go straight to your place. He said they'll meet us there. He has the analysis for the pills you two bought last night, and he wants you to start working on an antidote as soon as they get there with the information."

"How do they intend to manage this? Assuming I can even create an antidote, how are they going to get it into the hospital and administer it to that girl?"

As she spoke, Alessande became aware that someone was coming up behind them, and she turned to see that it was Greg Swayze. And he was still smiling.

"You both read very well. Excellent job."

"Thank you," Sailor said.

"It was the material," Alessande said. "It was excellent, too."

She turned on the Elven charm, planning to bedazzle, and so did Sailor, to the point that Alessande wasn't sure which one of them he was talking to when he starting speaking again.

"I was hoping that maybe I could see you for coffee or a drink," he said, smiling awkwardly. "Not that I'm the power when it comes to making casting decisions—I wouldn't want you to think I was holding that over you—but just…because."

"I suspect you have more power than you think," Alessande said. "But I'm saying yes because I think you're a nice guy, as well as talented."

Just then she saw that Declan was coming their way. Swayze noticed him, too.

"That's Declan Wainwright, isn't it? Owner of the Snake Pit? Is he here for one of you?"

"Declan is an old friend," Sailor said. "A very old friend."

"He's just picking us up—you know what parking in L.A. is like," Alessande added.

Declan offered a hand to Swayze and introduced himself.

Swayze smiled and reciprocated.

"Nice to meet you," Declan said. "Ladies, shall we?"

"Coffee tomorrow?" Swayze asked, looking at Alessande.

"How about noon. Do you know the Mystic Café?" she asked him.

"I do. I'll see you there."

He turned and went back to the audition room.

"A friend?" Declan asked, looking at Sailor. "A *very old* friend?"

She shrugged. "I didn't tell him how old."

"Not the point," Declan warned.

Slipping her arm through his and leaning against his shoulder, Sailor giggled. "Don't be jealous. I won't be meeting him, Alessande will. I think she'll be able to figure out what's going on with our screenwriter—if anything even is. Don't you?"

Declan only grunted. Behind them, Alessande felt a twinge of resentment; Declan should know that she was very adept at what she did.

"And besides," Sailor said, "I really would like a

part in that movie, and I think Alessande can make that happen for me."

As they walked out of the building, Alessande had the curious feeling of being watched. She turned around to look, but she didn't see anyone.

And yet she was certain that someone was observing them closely.

Chapter 7

Brigitte Hildegard was perched in the corner of one of the settees in the elegant room where they'd met before.

Alan was standing at the doorway, waiting, as the butler led Mark and Brodie in.

Charlaine Hildegard, who looked to be in her early thirties, was seated across from Brigitte. There was something about the way she sat there—in one of the high wingback chairs—that was distinctly imperial. She might be the cousin of the male heir in residence, but she was every inch the queen of her domain.

Her hair was darker than Brigitte's, her eyes a more intense blue. Her facial structure was classic—and her attitude was arrogance personified.

Neither she nor Brigitte rose as the men came into the room. Mark felt as if they had stepped back in time to Regency England. Charlaine waited regally for them to come and pay homage to her.

They obliged.

"Detectives, this is my cousin Charlaine. If you need to know something about the Hildegard family, Charlaine is the one to ask. And she has agreed to speak with you."

Mark refrained from clicking his heels, bowing and kissing the hand that was offered to him. He managed to grasp the hand—with its flawless manicure—and shake it. "Thank you so much for seeing us, and I apologize for the unpleasant nature of the topic we need to discuss with you, but, as I'm sure you're aware, two women are dead, and we believe that another was meant to be sacrificed upon your great-grandfather's tomb," he said.

Charlaine wrinkled her nose. "This is ever so distasteful," she said.

Yes, he thought, trying not to roll his eyes at her choice of words. Murder could be *ever so distasteful.*

"I do hope that you've found something with which to charge those people," she added.

"At the moment, Ms. Hildegard," Brodie said, "charges are pending."

"At least you have the perpetrators locked up," she said.

"I'm afraid they're out on their own recognizance at the moment," Brodie admitted.

"Goodness! What use are the police?" she asked.

"We believe that they don't really understand what was going on that night," Mark explained.

From her perch on the settee, Brigitte let out a soft groan. "Really, Detective, what was done to our family tomb, *that* is the *real* crime!"

Yes, to the Hildegard family, trespassing in their tomb might well appear to be a far greater crime than murder.

"Ms. Hildegard, according to newspaper articles of the time," Mark said, "your great-grandfather was a student of the occult, and he himself professed a belief that he could be brought back to life."

She smiled. "My great-grandfather was a show-man, Detective. He knew how to entertain, his… dabblings in the occult made him very good at entertaining. I assure you, we aren't hiding any ancient texts that hold the secrets to life and death—or life after death." She smiled at him. "As a vampire, you should know far more about that than any of us."

"I was born a vampire, Ms. Hildegard."

"Well, of course you were. But to the best of my knowledge, only vampires can come back from death in any way, and that's because, whether by bite or birth, their chemical makeup is different, so they're not really dead until they have their hearts staked or their heads chopped off." Her smiled deepened, but there was something taunting about it. "So, no, our family does not have any answers, and whatever performances my great-grandfather put on…well, they were just that. Performances. Now, as to the vandalism at my family's tomb...you *will* see that something is done, correct?"

"We'll do our best," Mark promised.

She waved a hand in the air. Like a queen, she was dismissing them.

"Thank you so much for speaking with us," Brodie told her.

Privately, Mark was wondering what the point of their trip had been, since she hadn't actually told them a thing.

"Not at all," she said. "You may, of course, call me at any time." She looked from Brodie to Mark, where her gaze lingered, as if she were judging him.

Mark smiled. "A pleasure to have met you."

As they left the Hildegard estate, Brodie turned to Mark and laughed. "You should ask her out. Maybe we could actually get some information from her that way."

"What?"

"Seriously. Did you see the way she was looking at you?"

"And you know that how? Did you do some kind of Elven mind read?"

Brodie shook his head. "No. I tried, of course. Thing is, she's an Other, and she knew she was going to meet a vampire and an Elven. She was prepared, careful not to let me make that kind of eye contact."

"That woman is scary," Mark said.

"Maybe, but she's still into you," Brodie said. He

punched Mark in the shoulder. "You should take one for the team. You're free, after all," he said cheerfully.

Free. Yes, he was. But, oddly, he didn't *feel* free. It had started with that freaky daydream at the cemetery.

And then…

Then, last night, he'd held her. Kissed her. And when he'd held her, when he'd kissed her…

No, I'm not free. I don't know why, but I'm not. Which was ridiculous. And he should be free, because, if he wasn't…

Again he saw the blood, running down the aisle as if it were a red velvet runner.…

"We're cops. I'm sure we can figure something else out," he said casually. "Come on, we've got to get to Alessande's house. A girl is dying. Alessande needs this lab report."

"Transymil is actually in the hemlock family," Alessande explained, dicing leaves to add to the potion she was making. "So you would probably treat it much the same way you would treat hemlock poisoning. Although…there's more here than just a hemlock derivative. Okay, let's go back to the beginning. Originally this drug was only known in the Otherworld. It comes from a plant grown solely in a small part of the world by the local Others."

"Go on," Mark said. "Say it. Vampires."

"Well, everything starts somewhere, and I swear,

I'm not looking to offend vampires," she said, gazing across the counter at him. His expression was amused, and she realized that he'd been baiting her.

He and Brodie had arrived half an hour ago. She'd immediately begun to study the report, and then had started formulating the potion she hoped would be an antidote. She realized that she was ridiculously ill at ease with Mark, especially right there in her house. It had been one thing to dream about a ridiculous wedding in which she was somehow intended to be a sacrifice—it was quite another to dream about having wanton sex with the man. The best antidote for her was to keep as busy as possible creating an antidote for Transymil.

Brodie, Sailor and Declan had just left, and she was all too aware of being alone with Mark.

"What's in there?" he asked, looking at the steaming pot on her stove.

"Simple things, mostly. Tannic acid, ground coffee, mustard and castor oils, and then some ingredients we Elven are particularly aware of. Fenweddin, persicle, bee leaf. And…" She paused, looking for a sharp knife. She glanced at him apologetically for a moment as she prepared to prick her finger. "…a drop of Elven blood. It has restorative properties."

"Do you want me to leave the room?" he asked, a slight edge to his voice. "Are you afraid I'll see that speck of blood and freak out, sink my fangs into you and drain you dry in a flash of uncontrollable desire?"

She felt a flush rising to her cheeks. She was very afraid that she wouldn't mind the *uncontrollable desire* part as long as he left the fangs out of it.

I don't even like him! she told herself.

But she did.

"Alessande, I've been on synthetic blood since I was born. My mother didn't even go for slaughterhouse blood, the way so many people did. She's a vegetarian," he told her.

"I'm sorry," she murmured. Then she pricked her finger and allowed three drops of blood to fall into the potion.

"What now?" he asked as she stirred the pot.

"Now, it needs about two hours to simmer," she said. "How are you and Brodie going to get this to her? She's in the hospital—and I'm assuming there's a police guard on her. If they're not Others…"

Mark nodded. "True. But Brodie and I are the lead detectives on the related murder case. We'll have no problem getting in."

"But you have to get this into her—unnoticed."

"I am a vampire," he reminded her.

"Right," Alessande said, and moved uneasily away from the stove. She looked out the window and breathed in the peace of her surroundings. Her house, which was actually a cabin, stood in a beautiful forested area. She needed the trees; Elven were tied to the earth. They hadn't come to the States until commercial flight had become common, because they couldn't survive in water for long, and even traveling on the water by ship was draining for them. In fact, if they were away from land for *too* long, they perished.

She glanced toward the bay window in her living room. An ornament hung there, a talisman for her people, a tree with roots so long that they grew upward toward the sky and joined with the branches.

She had always loved what she was; her people believed in learning and in healing, and they truly honored the earth.

But now she knew that she wasn't only Elven. Her biological father had been a Keeper.

"Are you all right?" Mark asked her.

"Of course." She lowered the heat on the potion so that it could simmer and covered the steaming pot. Nervously she looked at him. "Um, if there's something you need to do, feel free. You can come back in a couple hours when this is ready."

He shook his head. "Alessande, there is no way on earth that I'm going to leave you alone right now."

"You really don't need to worry. I doubt many people even know that this cabin is here."

He sighed, and actually seemed to be struggling for patience. "Alessande, I'm a cop. And as a cop you learn pretty quickly that if a bad guy wants to find someone, he does. I meant what I said. I'm not leaving you alone until this is over."

"Oh, well…we have two hours, then."

"What, that's it?" he asked.

"What do you mean?"

"No passionate demands that I leave? No insistence that you can take care of yourself, that you're not just Elven, you're destined to be a Keeper?" But he was smiling, and she loved that smile. Loved the way it made the gold flecks seem to burn in his eyes, loved the little dimple it caused to appear in just one cheek.

"No," she said simply. "So…what would you like to do? We can watch a movie, listen to some music. I have some board games around here somewhere."

She was startled when he walked over to stand beside her, just leaning against the counter, not quite touching her.

"We could have mad passionate sex," he said.

Her breath caught. "I, uh, I was under the impression that you didn't like me very much."

"Sad to say the truth about men and sex—any men, human, Other, anything in between—is that, on the one hand, liking someone doesn't really matter very much. But, on the other hand, you're very much mistaken. I do like you," he told her, humor still in his eyes. And then his voice changed, going soft and serious. "I like you *too* much."

She stared at him for a long moment. She wondered if it was just her, or if the *like* part didn't always matter that much with women, either—Elven, Other, human, whatever—not when the man was Mark, someone who moved with confidence, had the perfect physique, had the sexiest hint of huskiness in his voice and flecks of gold in his eyes.…

She moved into his arms, reaching up to touch his face.

"Movie, board game...hot passionate sex," she whispered. "Um, I think the third would be my choice."

This time *she* kissed *him*. She arched against him, rising on her toes, sliding her fingers down his cheek. Her lips touched his and their mouths parted, and, as their tongues met, she felt as if the world around her grew electrified, or maybe it was just her...just the impossible heat of him filling her.

He wound his arms around her, drawing her closer and closer. His hands slid along her back to her buttocks, and then she was flush against him and wishing she could feel his flesh against hers. He seemed to feel the same way. He started to rip at his shirt, then remembered he was wearing a gun and stepped back, looking at her apologetically as he removed his holster.

No sooner had he set the gun on the counter than her hands were on his buttons and his were on the soft silk of her blouse. They fumbled with each other's clothing as their lips met again. She spoke against his mouth as they leaned against the counter. "I do have a bedroom."

"Oh, yeah?"

"Yeah."

She caught him by the arm and started to lead him toward it, but he stopped, and for a moment she was confused. Had she acted too quickly? Was she crazy? Were they just playing some kind of ridiculous game and he'd thought better of it?

But he'd only stopped for his gun. "Wherever we go…it comes with us."

She drew him into the bedroom.

She loved her room. It was beautifully paneled in natural woods. Her bed was in an alcove, the head- and footboards and posts carved with leaves.

He pulled back for a second to look. "Wow."

"Too much?" she asked.

"No, just…wow."

He laid the holster on the bedside table and fell with her onto her mattress. And when they landed, he smiled down at her. "I think I've gone a little crazy, because right now I could devour you like a rabid werewolf," he said.

"Elven have no fear of such things," she assured him.

"Ah, fearless Elven," he teased. Their mouths melded again. Her shoes, his shoes, hit the floor, and the rest of their clothing soon followed, until at last they lay together as she had craved, flesh to flesh. They tangled breathlessly in a long and lasting kiss, and when his lips broke from hers, they traveled her body restlessly, moving over her throat and brushing slowly against her shoulder. His kisses poured over her breasts and rib cage and abdomen. She burned and writhed against him, amazed at the strength of the need ripping through her. How long had it been? She didn't know, didn't remember, didn't care. She had tended all through her long life to be discriminating; she'd seldom indulged in affairs. But here he was, majestic and beautiful, and when he smiled...

This was more than just physical need. She ached to touch more than his flesh; she longed for everything inside of him. She could read minds....

She wanted to read his *soul*.

He was a consummate and inventive lover, taking his time, taking luxurious care, kissing, caressing... making love in a way she hadn't thought possible. He knew where to touch, how to touch, where to kiss, when to tease...and when to become so intimate that she felt as if the wonder inside her would boil over.

And then he would bring her back down ever so slightly, giving her the opportunity to touch him in turn, to press herself closer and closer, to bathe his shoulders with kisses and serenade him with moans raggedly drawn from her lips.

His body was solid, strong and vital. His lips laved her abdomen, traveled lower and teased between her thighs until she thought she would go mad.

And then he was above her, in her, and her arms were wrapped around him. She stared into his eyes and felt again that fire blazing through her with a wild vengeance. She whispered incoherently, and felt the power of her own passion and desire as she responded to him. It was beautiful; it was incredible. He led her upward to a place she'd never been to before, and the carved forest around them seemed to amplify every sensation, make it part of the earth.

and air. She felt his movements, the sweet thrusts, the rhythm, and it was as if her world spun on its axis, making her dizzy with want. The pace of their loving grew frantic, stars seeming to blaze across the ceiling above her as she climaxed with a volatile shudder. She felt the rigidity of his muscles as he thrust deeply into her, and then held, and stayed, and finally lay carefully against her and pulled her to her side as they both cooled down and relearned how to breathe, still entwined, still together.

It wasn't like her dream. It was better. It was real. And in the aftermath she drew strength from the wood of her bed and the walls of her home. She had wanted him—desperately. It wouldn't have mattered if they *hadn't* been here. But it was somehow better because they *had* been.

She lay against him, her cheek resting on his chest, still in awe of the experience. She was sure that she felt his heart hammering, even as she was certain that she'd felt warmth from him earlier. Vampires, she'd always heard, were cold. Their hearts did not beat; they did not breathe. They hungered; they did not love.

"I really do like it," he murmured.

"Sex?"

"Well, yes, that, too—but I was thinking of your bed."

"I'm glad." Her fingers moved over his chest. "I can feel your heart."

"Of course."

"You're a vampire."

"My heart exists—why else would you kill a vampire by staking him in the heart?" He was stroking her hair, lulling her.

"Good point," she murmured. "I always thought…"

"I know," he said huskily. "It's so easy to believe the myths, to think that what we know about those who are different from us is right."

"I never had any negative assumptions about vampires."

"Oh, you are such a liar," he said, but his tone was light, and his fingers continued to move gently through her hair.

"I was aggravated," she said.

"You were obnoxious."

"I was…scared." She sat up and leaned against his chest, seeking his eyes. "I knew what I was doing that night. I walked in with my eyes wide-open. I just didn't suspect that—"

He caught her shoulders. "That's just it. That's where Brodie and I are ahead of the game. We're cops. We've learned that you can never *suspect* everything that might happen, so you have to be prepared for everything. Don't get me wrong. I don't think that we are invincible or infallible. But—"

"But I might have been fine without you. I am excellent at teleporting."

He smiled. "I believe you. But admit it—you,

were really just pissed because you were scared and I saved your life."

"That might have a hint of truth," she said.

His smiled broadened. "I guess I'll take that for now."

She didn't speak. She leaned low against him and they kissed.

Once again…

She hadn't really *suspected*.

One kiss, that kiss. The room, the warmth of the wood around her—the searing heat of the man beneath her. One kiss, that kiss, and suddenly they were touching feverishly and making love again, until finally, exhausted and spent, she lay beside him in silence. Then, as he started to ease away, she bolted up. "The potion!"

Mark laughed, a husky, easy sound. "It's all right. It's only been two hours since we came in here."

She looked at him, startled. "You know that?"

"I do."

She leaped out of bed, heedless of her nudity, comfortable with it. She was an earth creature. In a different time, when people lived far apart and she had lived in dense woods, she had frequently walked around naked. Her body was a part of the earth, like the woods she loved so dearly, and she cared for it well. And with Mark…she felt an ease and a sense of comfort.

But she didn't get very far, because he pulled her back.

"Hey—the potion."

"Everything's all right."

"The potion," she repeated firmly.

She left the bedroom and hurried to the kitchen. She lifted the cover and stirred the contents. The consistency was right. The tiny drops of her blood gave it a slight tint of mauve. She quickly turned off the heat and removed the pot from the range so that it could cool. She dug into the shelf behind the sink, finding the right size vials to hold the finished product.

She turned and saw that Mark was standing right behind her, already dressed, his holster in place. He slipped his jacket on, hiding the weapon.

"You look like a nymph. A glorious tall nymph. Really tall."

"The nymphs might take exception to that," she told him.

He grinned, reaching for one of the vials.

"No, no, get away!" she told him, batting his hand with a spoon. "I have to get this done."

"I like you this way—I mean, I *really* like you this way," he told her. "But I'll fill the vials. You get dressed. We'll rush one of these to the hospital, then I'll take you back to the House of the Rising Sun."

Alessande quickly ran to her room to dress, leaving him to his work. When she came out, he'd finished his self-appointed task.

She looked at the vials. "Good job," she said.

"Hey, even *I* can pour liquid into a bottle."

"You never know," she said lightly, taking one of

the vials. She swallowed the contents quickly, before he could stop her.

He immediately grabbed the vial, staring at her as if she'd lost her mind. "Why did you do that?" he demanded.

"We can't give it to a dying girl if it causes a reaction in me."

His expression was thunderous. "First of all, you're Elven, so its effect on you could be completely different from its effect on her. And second, what if you *do* have an adverse reaction?"

She smiled. "You can stop worrying. I know what's in it, and it can't possibly do more than give me a stomachache. It *should* make me feel good—cleansed. So if we get to the hospital and I'm still fine, then it's safe to give it to the girl who was poisoned."

"But—"

"Trust me, Mark, please. Have a little faith that I know potions. After all, you're the one who asked me to do this."

He still looked grim. "It has to work, and we have to give it to her. If something from our world doesn't save her—then she's dead."

He was right, she knew. And though she didn't know the girl in the hospital and she didn't feel the same desperation she did over Regina Johnson, she believed that all life was precious. She lived by that precept just as she honored the Code of Silence.

"I'll carry the vials in my purse," she said.

"I'll put one in my pocket, just so we'll be covered in case that big bird is flying around somewhere," he said.

She smiled and leaned into him, kissing him. "Now let's go," she said as he groaned in arousal. "We have a girl to save."

Twenty minutes later they reached the hospital. Mark pulled the Mustang's replacement, a Charger, into a spot reserved for police so they didn't have to spend another twenty minutes looking for a place to park.

His badge got them quickly through to where they needed to be. Outside Chelsea Rose's room, a uniformed officer sat reading a paper. He stood up quickly when he saw Mark. "Detective Valiente."

"Dave, hello. How is Miss Rose doing?"

Dave shook his head. "The doctors don't give me reports, but, from what I've heard, she's hanging in, yet with no real change. It's a shame. Pretty girl. So young."

He looked questioningly at Alessande and cleared his throat.

"Alessande Salisbrooke," Mark said, "meet one of L.A.'s finest, David Robbins. David, Alessande."

"Nice to meet you," Dave said and shook her hand, staring at her. He seemed to be in awe. Probably because she was three inches taller than he was.

"I'm going to go in and take a look at Miss Rose, Dave," Mark said.

"Sure. Except Miss Salisbrooke can't go in. Only

family, medical personnel, the lieutenant, you and Brodie—that's what I've been told," Dave said firmly. "She's welcome to stay out here with me, though."

Alessande watched as Mark casually moved directly in front of Dave and looked into his eyes. "Dave, she needs to come in with me."

Dave stared back at Mark, a little glassy-eyed, and nodded. "She needs to go in with you."

Mark quickly set a hand on Alessande's back, urging her into the room.

Chelsea Rose lay in bed, an IV dripping fluid into a vein in her arm. Oxygen entered her system through a tube. She looked small and frail, so pathetic. She was a stranger, and yet she touched Alessande's heart and left her feeling a little guilty that her passion to save her friend had been greater than her desire to save this girl.

They had to stop what was going on, and she realized now that she never could have done it alone.

Mark walked up to the bed. He touched the unconscious girl's lips, parting them slightly.

"You'll choke her," Alessande said worriedly.

But Mark shook his head. "No, I'll lift her head so that it rolls down her throat." He drew out the vial and handed it to Alessande. "Pour it as far back in her throat as you can."

She nodded and glanced nervously toward the door.

"Don't worry. Come on. Your turn to have some faith," he told her, offering her a wry smile.

She nodded. "I have faith," she assured him.

"Then quit looking at the door."

Alessande was impressed with the way he gently lifted and cradled the girl's head. She parted the girl's parched lips and tilted the vial, pouring the potion into Chelsea's mouth. In an involuntary reflex triggered by the liquid's passage, the girl swallowed.

"Perfect," Mark murmured. He laid Chelsea's head back down on the pillow, took the vial from Alessande and pocketed it.

"And now?" Alessande said, whispering.

"Now we leave—and pray it works," he said.

Alessande hesitated, looking at the girl. So young, so slight...so sunken. She touched Chelsea's cheek.

"Live!" she said softly. "Please live."

She thought she saw the girl stir and a slight flush color her cheeks.

"Alessande," Mark said.

As she turned and followed him to the door, she heard something like a deep breath. Perhaps a long sigh.

Maybe, just maybe, the girl was going to live.

Chapter 8

They arrived en masse at the Snake Pit and were seated at a perfectly situated table along one wall. Mark positioned himself where he could see anyone entering the room. Alessande was next to him, with Brodie, Sailor, Mick and Barrie taking the other chairs. Declan was doing his duty as owner and host, and Rhiannon sat on the low dais, playing the piano.

An intriguing assortment of Hollywood royalty was present already, several of them involved with *Death in the Bowery*. Tonight Sailor had pointed out costume designer Katrina Manville seated at a rear table with director Taylor Haywood, associate producer Tilda Lyons and casting director Milly Caulfield.

They had just ordered drinks from a lovely young were-cat waitress when Brodie's phone rang.

Mark watched across the table as he answered it. "That's great," Brodie said after a few seconds, then listened for a moment more and rang off.

"Edwards?" Mark asked him.

"Yep. He said Chelsea is still extremely weak, but she's out of the coma. The last thing she remembers is that she and her boyfriend—Steiner—had decided to score something so they could have a fun night. Her mind is still fuzzy and she's barely able to speak, but we can interview her tomorrow."

"It worked," Alessande breathed. "It really worked."

Mark smiled at her. "Yes, you saved her life."

"Don't look now," Brodie said, interrupting them, "but the plot thickens."

Mark turned casually. The Hildegard family had just entered the room. Alan was the epitome of L.A. casual in a tan sports jacket and perfectly creased trousers; Brigitte was wearing a slinky blue cocktail dress, and Charlaine...Charlaine looked regal in a long spangled creation. He wondered if she was going to offer her hand to Declan so he could kiss it.

She refrained. Instead Declan greeted her with a kiss on each cheek, Continental style. Alan Hildegard said something to Declan, who indicated the group from *Death in the Bowery*.

"Who is it?" Alessande asked softly.

"The Hildegards. Alan, his sister Brigitte, and their cousin Charlaine," he explained softly.

"No Jimmy," Brodie said.

"Who is Jimmy?" Sailor asked.

"The butler," Mark told her.

"I was kidding," Brodie said. "They'd never bring the butler."

"How rude of them," Alessande said.

"Not to that trio," Mark said.

"Don't judge too harshly," Mick said, smiling. "I mean, we don't really know them. Perhaps they're lovely people."

"I *should* know them, since they're shapeshifters," Barrie said. "My domain."

"I'm pretty sure Declan only knows them because they come to the club," Sailor said. "I've never met any of them."

"And they're joining the film crew of *Death in the Bowery,*" Mark said, "so there definitely is a connection." He glanced at Barrie. "Well, you started the interviews, so you should continue."

"I can't just walk up to their table," Barrie said.

"I can," Mark told her. "Give them a minute to get settled."

"I'd wait another minute if I were you," Alessande said softly.

"Why?"

She indicated the doorway, where Declan was busy greeting someone else.

Greg Swayze.

"Well, this *is* getting interesting," Mick murmured.

"I could become a fly and buzz on over," Barrie suggested.

"No," Mick told her. "They're shapeshifters, they might suspect."

"Only the Hildegards are shapeshifters," Barrie argued. "If I were to settle around one of the others…"

"Mick is right. Too dangerous," Mark said. He stood before they could argue, pretending to stretch and then notice the Hildegards.

Charlaine was looking his way. She smiled. He pretended to be startled to see her, then walked over to her table. "Hello. Nice to see you," he said, smiling at them one by one, first Alan, followed by Brigitte—and then Charlaine.

"Detective. What a surprise to see you here," she said.

"I come fairly often. Declan is a friend," he explained.

"Well, of course," Charlaine said softly, and he heard in her tone an acknowledgment that it was natural for one Other, especially a cop, to know another, especially someone with a public profile like Declan's. "Let me introduce you to our friends. This is Katrina Manville—"

"Of course. The renowned costume designer," Mark said.

"Pleasure. I've seen you here before," Katrina said.

"And Taylor Haywood, Milly Caulfield, Greg Swayze and Tilda Lyons," Charlaine said. "And, of course, you know my cousins Alan and Brigitte."

"Detective Mark Valiente," Alan said, introducing him in return. "He's working on that dreadful business that occurred at our family tomb," he added, as if to explain why he would know a civil servant.

"Nice to meet you all. Actually, I'm not on duty tonight. I'm just here with a few friends who I believe know you," Mark said, smiling at the film crew. "They're actresses."

"Oh?" Swayze said, looking in the direction Mark had come from, but there were people in the way, blocking his view.

"Sailor Gryffald and Alessande Salisbrooke," Mark said. "They auditioned for a role in your new film."

Swayze nodded. "Alessande is here? And Ms. Gryffald, of course."

"Right over there," Mark said.

He was surprised when Swayze stood right away. "Excuse me," he mumbled, and was gone.

"Both of them read very well," Haywood told Mark.

"The girl is playing a fox-trot, a real fox-trot," Charlaine said. "I do love a fox-trot. And how often does one get the chance these days? Detective, you're already standing. Do you dance?" she asked, a mischievous smile on her lips.

"I do, yes," he said, offering her a hand. "And I'd be delighted if you'd join me," he said.

Charlaine took his hand and rose, smiling sweetly. He excused them to the others and led her out to the floor.

She slid into his arms easily, holding her head and shoulders at a perfect—very lofty—angle. She seemed to savor the music like a sensual touch, allowing her head to fall back for a moment, her eyes closed. Her fingers moved on his shoulders, and then her eyes opened and she looked at him. "Lovely, Detective. Few men can dance these days. Really dance. But then, you *have* been around for a while, haven't you? Long enough to remember when dancing took true finesse, and when manners and courtesy were to be admired."

"Yes, I have been around awhile," he said.

"Vampires tend to be so magnetic," she murmured.

"I'm glad you think so," he said.

"Have you made any headway, Detective? My cousins are quite distraught, you know."

"We're searching for the truth of the situation, Ms. Hildegard," he said. "And I promise you, we'll find it."

"You suspect my family has something to do with this, don't you?" She smiled, pursing her lips slightly. "You're quite wrong."

He changed the subject. "Your cousin Alan led

me to believe he'd passed on filming Greg Swayze's screenplay."

"Oh, he *did* pass."

"But given his presence here tonight, it seems he *is* involved with the filming?"

She smiled. "This is Hollywood, Detective. 'Involved' can mean so many things. Alan loved the screenplay, and though he couldn't afford to option it himself, he made some calls to ensure that it went to a studio that would do it justice. In doing that, it seems, he has befriended Mr. Swayze. And since this is one of our favorite places, when we decided to take Greg and his associates out, this seemed like just the place to suggest."

"I see." He *did* see. Alan *was* still involved in the project at the heart of his murder case.

She laughed softly. "Oh, no, Detective. You don't see at all. So," she added softly, "you will keep investigating and…coming round, won't you?"

"I may need your help again, yes," he said.

"I'll be delighted to give it."

As she spoke, another couple swept by them.

Alessande—and Greg Swayze.

Swayze didn't even notice them; his eyes were only on Alessande. Mark couldn't help but feel a twinge of jealousy.

He tried to dance closer to them without Charlaine realizing his purpose, using his heightened hearing to eavesdrop.

Swayze certainly wasn't telling Alessande any

deep, dark secrets. He was waxing eloquent about the intelligence, the courage and the passion of the heroine of *Death in the Bowery*.

"Are you a movie buff, Detective?" Charlaine asked him.

"Not particularly."

"But…those actresses are your friends, right?"

"Yes."

"Keepers!" Charlaine said with a hiss.

He grinned at that. "You don't like Keepers?"

"We don't *need* Keepers," she said. "We need rights, the right to be free to be what we are."

"But Keeper law allows for that. It's the very point of their existence."

"Ah, spoken like a true vampire," she said. "Shifters are…different." She shrugged. "Your friend—the Elven cop. They're the least powerful, aren't they? The Elven. The most like human beings."

"I like to think that we all, Others and humans, share something that binds us."

"Oh?"

"The soul, the belief in right and wrong that allows us to make moral choices rather than being driven by selfishness and greed."

She laughed. "But, Detective, this is Hollywood. Everyone out here is soulless, don't you know?"

The music ended. Applause filled the room.

"Thank you for the dance," Charlaine said.

"No, thank you," Mark replied.

He noted Greg Swayze was still with Alessande.

They were standing and chatting by the table. Alessande seemed to be introducing him to the rest of the group.

"Intrigued by the screenwriter?" Charlaine asked archly. "Or intrigued by his interest in your friend?"

Mark looked down at her. "I think he's exceptionally talented."

She laughed softly. "Come, take me over to meet the rest of your friends."

"You must know Barrie Gryffald—she's the Keeper of the Laurel Canyon shapeshifters."

"I know *of* Barrie Gryffald," she said.

"She's also a reporter, and she's looking to give the movie a boost," Mark said. "No doubt she can send some publicity your cousin's way, as well."

"Please, Detective! Investigate us all you like, but don't mistake me for a fool. Her interest is purely in the Hildegard connection to *Death in the Bowery*."

"Ah, but if it's okay that we investigate you all we like, why not help Barrie and let your cousin and the family business benefit, as well?" he asked.

She tipped her head to the side as she mulled over the question. "You're right, the publicity will be quite beneficial." She offered him a seductive smile and moved closer to him. "So let your friend play cat and mouse with Greg and the crew. I don't mind at all if *you* 'investigate' *me*. Some of my favorite friends and…*investigators* through the years have been vampires."

"I'm pleased to hear it," he said.

"Now introduce me around," she said, her mischievous smile intact.

He led her to the table, where the men rose as he made the introductions. Barrie acknowledged Charlaine with a smile and said she was pleased to meet her at last, and Charlaine admitted that she seldom attended council meetings, preferring to live quietly, out of the mainstream of the Otherworld.

Throughout the conversation, Swayze remained silent, a besotted smile on his face as he watched Alessande. Eventually Charlaine took his arm and led him back to their table.

"Anything?" Mark asked as he sat back down.

"I'd say Swayze has a crush the size of Texas on our Alessande," Brodie said.

Mark leaned forward and said, "They're having coffee tomorrow. He wants to talk to her about the lead role in the upcoming movie."

"Go figure," Sailor said, but she was smiling as she shrugged.

"Sailor, I have no interest in that role or any other," Alessande said.

"Don't be silly—better one of us gets the part," Sailor said.

Alessande smiled. "But this opportunity could be really important for you. I just want to find Regina and stop what's happening before anyone else dies."

"We're going to find Regina," Sailor assured her. "And we will stop this, but I confess I wouldn't mind landing a role, too," Sailor said, grinning. "That would mean a real paycheck—one that could mean I won't have to wait on so many tables."

They all smiled at that. Alessande turned to Mark. "Speaking of crushes…"

"She's right," Mick said, looking at Mark with a teasing light in his eyes. "Our shape-shifting beauty Ms. Charlaine Hildegard seems to be eating you alive with her eyes."

"We don't have a date for coffee," he said.

"I don't think it's coffee she wants," Barrie commented dryly.

"Keep an eye on the Hildegard crew," Mark told the table. "Alessande, want to take a walk?"

"Sure," she said, but there was a question in her eyes.

"We're going back to see Digger," he told her.

"Ah," she said.

"You'll follow him tonight?" Brodie asked.

Mark nodded.

"Just give me a buzz if you need me," Brodie said.

"I think Barrie and I should hit the research trail," Mick said. "We can take Sailor home with us. Declan owns the place, so he has to stay, and it makes sense for you to stay, too, Brodie, since you're engaged to Rhiannon."

"It's a good plan," Brodie said. "I think I'll circulate downstairs and see if I can pick up any good gossip. You never know what might turn out to be relevant."

"Works for me," Mark said.

"Not for me," Sailor protested. "I'm staying here. I can hang out up here and see if the Hildegards and their film friends get up to anything suspicious."

"That makes sense," Alessande said. "Especially because it would be natural for Sailor to slide into conversations with any of the film crew, since she's a working actress."

"An almost-working actress," Sailor said.

"A wonderful actress," Brodie assured her.

At that, Mick, Barrie, Alessande and Mark made a show of saying goodbye, leaving Brodie and Sailor still at the table and pausing on the way out to make a show of thanking Declan. Outside, they split up, Barrie and Mick retrieving Mick's car from the valet, while Mark and Alessande headed down the street.

As they walked, retracing their steps from the previous night, Mark said, "So, did you work any Elven magic on our boy Swayze?" He sounded jealous, he realized.

She looked up at him, smiling. "No, actually, I didn't. Believe it or not, he's genuinely attracted to me."

"Oh, I believe it."

"What about you? Use any vampire glamour on the lovely Charlaine?"

He shook his head. "Of course, I'm not having coffee with Charlaine Hildegard."

"Coffee seems quite tame, really, doesn't it? It was pretty evident what she wants from you."

He grinned. "Jealous?" he teased her.

"Not at all," she said. "What's important here is solving this case and finding Regina."

"Of course."

"Are *you* jealous?" she asked.

"You bet," he told her.

She smiled at that. "Okay, so I'm a *little* bit jealous. More than that, actually. I'd like to smack her in her smug, overly made-up face."

He laughed and pulled her close. "You know…she doesn't compare to you," he said softly.

He wasn't sure what she would have answered, because she suddenly tensed and said, "There's Digger!"

He was leaning against a building, smoking. They approached him, and he instantly straightened, looking worried. "Hey, I have a prescription," he said. "It's for medicinal use!"

"Sure, whatever," Mark said. "We were looking to, um, see what you have tonight."

Digger squinted and looked at the two of them. "Oh, yeah." He frowned. "Cool to see you again."

"You sound surprised to see us," Alessande told him.

"No, uh, no. But—" He stopped and looked around, as if afraid someone might overhear him, but after a moment he seemed satisfied that no one else was around. "That was some pretty powerful stuff I gave you. I don't usually get repeat customers so quickly."

"We want another dose," Mark said.

"I, um, don't have any more right now," Digger said. "I mean, I can get them. I can get them for you by tomorrow night."

"If that's really the best you can do…" Alessande said regretfully.

"It's the best, I swear it."

"Whatever," Mark said, then sighed and slipped an arm around Alessande. "Come on, honey, we're going to have to wait."

"But it will be worth it!" Digger called after them as they walked away.

"What do we do now?" Alessande asked Mark as soon as they were out of sight.

"You been practicing your shape-shifting?"

"I feel pretty confident," she said.

"Want to do a bat?" he asked. "I would suggest a wolf, but that's far too obvious for the streets of L.A."

She grinned. "Yeah, I can do a bat. What then?"

"Police work. We perch somewhere—and we wait. And we see where he leads us."

They rounded a corner into an alley. Mark went first, willing the change in his mind. He turned to smoke and then flapped his way up to a terrace in perfect bat form.

Alessande followed. She was good, he had to admit; she looked like the real deal.

He waited for her to feel comfortable with the change. They he flew down toward the street, looking for Digger.

They were not disappointed.

Digger was leaning against the building again, another joint in his hands. Mark rested on a rooftop, Alessande followed, and they settled down to wait together.

Waiting. It was one of the most tedious parts of his job.

He found himself thinking about the night he and Brodie had waited to burst into the Hildegard tomb. He was still troubled by the daydream or vision or whatever it was that he'd had that night. Alessande had been featured in it, though he'd yet to meet her at that time.

And now…

Now he knew her, and the vision was even more disturbing.

He told himself that he didn't need to be so worried. Not at this time anyway. There was no blood wedding on the horizon. They were bats, perched on a building, watching. And waiting.

At last they saw someone approaching Digger. Mark strained to see—not easy when he was in bat form.

It was a man, a tall man. He was wearing a trench coat despite the fact that the night was warm and there wasn't even a hint of rain in the air.

The man stopped in front of Digger, who managed to shrug his way out of his smoke-induced haze, straighten and begin talking to the man with a great deal of enthusiasm.

The man was angry. He smacked Digger against

the wall and, as Mark watched, pulled a knife from an inner pocket of his trench coat and raised it.

Mark flew down in a fury, moving as quickly as he could. He realized Alessande was at his side, moving swiftly in perfect unison.

Mark crashed purposefully into the attacker's arm. The knife missed Digger, striking the stucco facade of the building instead.

Digger twisted away and screamed, then turned and ran.

As the tall man raised his knife again, Mark took human form and grasped the man's arm, wrestling him to the ground. The knife went flying. Alessande, also in human form, went for the weapon.

The man was no match for Mark's strength, but as they struggled he managed to pop a pill into his mouth. As he swallowed, Mark was able at last to get a good look at his face.

It was Jimmy—the Hildegard butler.

"Jimmy!" he gasped.

Jimmy only stared back at him, not saying a word, as his lips started to draw back and he began to gag.

Mark realized that he hadn't swallowed something hallucinogenic.

He'd taken poison.

"No!" Mark roared, trying to wedge his fingers into Jimmy's mouth to keep him from choking.

Too late. Foam spewed from between Jimmy's lips.

Jimmy died before him, choking and writhing in pain.

Then…nothing.

Mark pulled out his phone to call Brodie, and, as he punched in the number, he looked around and saw that Digger was gone.

And so was Alessande.

Chapter 9

For someone who was so stoned, Digger could move.

Luckily Alessande could outrun almost anyone, including other Elven, simply because she loved to run and did it often.

But he had a head start.

Even so, she had no trouble chasing him down and overtaking him in the alley where she and Mark had transformed, and she certainly had no trouble tackling him to the ground. As she straddled him, he raised his arms over his face screaming, "Don't hurt me! Please, don't hurt me!"

"I'm not going to hurt you, Digger."

He screamed again, like a baby, or a cat with its tail caught in a door.

"Digger! I am *not* going to hurt you!"

He began to whimper.

"Listen to me. Get it through your head that I'm not going to hurt you—but you *are* going to answer some questions."

"What? What do you want to know?" he asked.

"Those pills you sold us the other night. Where did you get them? That man—"

"What, are you stupid?"

"All right, maybe I *am* going to hurt you."

"No, no, I'm sorry, I'm sorry—stop! You saw the man. The man who attacked me. That was the man who was giving me the pills to sell. Where the hell did you come from anyway? Oh, man, I'm so messed up."

"Digger, I need to know about the man."

"What's to know? He came down to the streets and found me—said he had the best stuff, stuff no one else had. He said I could walk away a rich man just by being selective, by finding couples to sell the stuff to. I mean, people didn't come back for more, not until you two, but no one wanted their money back, either. He's the one who knew about the stuff, honest. I was just trying to make a buck. I'm a salesman, that's all."

"Who is he, Digger?"

He opened his mouth to answer, and then his eyes suddenly went huge.

Alessande tried to turn around—to see what Digger had seen.

But even as she realized there was someone, something, behind her, she felt the air move, felt something heavy slam against her skull. For a moment she fought the dizziness that seized her. But the dust motes before her eyes began to dance, and, when she keeled over, she was dimly aware of Digger's scream as it faded away.

"Alessande!"

As Mark stood and shouted her name, Brodie came running down the street toward him.

"What the hell's going on?" Brodie asked. He looked at Jimmy, lying facedown on the sidewalk. "Who's that, and what happened to him?"

"It's Jimmy—the Hildegard butler. He took something before I could stop him. Cyanide, maybe. Call an ambulance—I'm going to find Alessande. Did you pass her?" he asked Brodie frantically.

Brodie shook his head. "No, but go. I've got this."

Mark tore off in the direction he recalled seeing Digger take, hoping Alessande had followed the dealer.

He almost passed the alley, but some instinct told him not to.

Where did a man run when he was terrified of the cops?

Into the shadows.

He turned on a dime and raced into the alley.

Time seemed to stop when he saw her; his body was paralyzed, his heart in his throat. She was lying, blond hair tumbled all around her, on the dirty pavement of the alley near a Dumpster.

Digger was there, too, flat on the ground in a pool of blood.

He raced to Alessande's side, falling to his knees. Even as fear numbed him, he reached for her, and she groaned softly.

"Alessande!"

Carefully, he cradled her in his arms. Her eyes opened to meet his, as blue-green, as large, as engulfing, as the sea. He felt life return to his limbs.

"Alessande," he said again.

"Mark!" she cried. Then she turned and saw Digger, and a gasp of horror escaped her. "Oh, Mark, I failed… I was… I should have seen what was coming, I should have saved him. Oh, God, I should have—" She broke off, a soft choking sound escaping her.

"Alessande, stop, there was no saving Digger any more than I could stop Jimmy from taking that pill," he said firmly.

"Jimmy?" She looked at him vaguely.

"Jimmy—the man who attacked Digger—was the Hildegards' butler."

She blinked. "The Hildegards' butler?" she said hesitantly.

"Sit still. I need to call an ambulance."

He heard the sound of sirens and realized Brodie had called in Jimmy's death.

"No ambulance," she said. "Please."

"But you're hurt."

"I want to get out of here. Take me back to the House of the Rising Sun. I can heal myself. And I can't bear to go to the police station again, trying to say what I need to say but holding back so anyone who's not an Other won't hear."

She was right, he realized.

"You didn't see who attacked you?" he asked.

She shook her head and looked over at Digger.

"Don't," he told her. "It was fast. Looks like they knocked you out of the way and killed him quickly."

"I have to get out of here."

"Can you teleport? Do you have the strength?" He could hear the ambulance and backup cop cars blaring their way down the street.

She nodded.

"Get to Castle House. Barrie and Mick should be there. Go quickly—and then lie down and heal."

"I will," she promised him.

She took his face in her hands and kissed him quickly, then disappeared.

And even there, in the presence of death, he felt her warmth, her touch, lingering on his lips.

Alessande materialized in the dining room of Castle House almost on top of Barrie. She and Mick had gone into research mode; they had old newspapers and spreadsheets fanned out on the table next to their laptop computers.

"Alessande!" Barrie cried. "Oh, no, look at you—you're bleeding."

"Just a little bang on the head," Alessande said. "I'm fine, really."

She wasn't, though, and she knew it. She was shaking. She'd been afraid she would lose it in the middle of teleporting, that she would wind up in molecular pieces somewhere, or simply flat on her back in the middle of the freeway, a semi bearing down on her.

Mick walked over, took hold of her shoulders and looked deeply into her eyes. "Are you sure you're all right?"

She nodded and quickly explained what had happened, rubbing the knot at the back of her head and already feeling the pain subside.

"The butler," Barrie mused. "Someone else for us to investigate. Now sit down. I'll brew some tea and then tell you what Mick and I have discovered. The public record is full of information if you know where to look."

"Yes, sit," Mick told her, pulling out a chair. He lifted her hair to inspect the damage. "Glutton for punishment," he told her.

"No, just so intent on trying to get information that I didn't hear someone coming up behind me. I should have suspected that Digger's attacker might not have come alone."

Just then Barrie returned with a silver tea service

and three cups. Mick repeated what Alessande had told him as Barrie poured the tea.

"Mark and Brodie are going to be hurting when they get back," Barrie said.

"Why?" Alessande asked.

"Wolfie—sorry, that's just my nickname for Lieutenant Edwards—is going to ream the two of them out. More deaths are not going to look good for the LAPD—especially when one of them's connected to a family as prominent as the Hildegards."

"But that's not their fault," Alessande said indignantly.

"Don't worry," Mick said reassuringly. "Brodie and Mark have both weathered worse. It's no easy task, being an Other and a cop, but they've done it for a lot of years. They'll be fine."

"Drink some tea—that always helps any situation," Barrie said. "Then take a hot shower. By the time you're done, the rest of the crew should be back, and we can explain what we found out once, instead of five or six times."

"But now I'm curious," Alessande protested.

"We have a few more connections to make, so give us time, okay?" Barrie said.

Alessande had to admit that she did feel scraped up and filthy. As if she'd been rolling in an alley.

Well, she had been.

"All right—I'll be back down in a little while." She finished off her cup of tea in a swallow, feeling it fill her with strength as it always did.

Then she stood and headed for the stairs to the second level of Castle House and her comfortable guest room.

Stepping into a shower was wonderful.

She only wished that…

She wished that Mark was with her.

As the hot water washed over her, she marveled at how quickly things could change. But she also found herself thinking about her strange dream again, her dream of a wedding in which everything was beautiful…

…until the blood started to flow, as rich a crimson as the velvet runner that covered the aisle to the altar.

And the memory made her shiver, despite the hot water cascading over her.

Mark was grateful to work with a partner like Brodie.

While he stood there in the alley receiving a good reaming-out from Lieutenant Edwards, Brodie was at his side, even though Mark had made it plain that Brodie had arrived on the scene after Jimmy had offed himself and Digger had been murdered.

"Let me get this straight. You were waiting to see what Digger was going to do—where he was going to get more of the drug?" Edwards said.

"Yes," Mark replied.

"Then this guy walks up to Digger and tries to kill him—and when you manage to stop him, he kills himself?"

"Yes."

"And then Digger ran into an alley and got murdered by someone else?" Edwards's tone was growing increasingly skeptical.

"Yes."

"So now they're both dead."

Mark nodded.

"Who killed Digger?" Edwards asked.

"I don't know," Mark admitted.

"Lieutenant, you know as well as we do that it could have been anyone," Brodie interjected. "Jimmy was obviously acting on behalf of someone else. He came to check up on Digger and found out he'd been selling to Mark—a cop. Whoever is employing him—and we can't be one hundred percent sure that's the Hildegards, even though they're certainly the most likely suspects—had Jimmy's complete loyalty or abject fear. He chose to die an agonizing death rather than face his employer and admit to failure."

"Which suggests an Other," Mark said.

"Maybe not—don't kid yourself. Human beings could teach the Others a lot about torture and cruelty," Edwards said softly. He shook his head, looking from Mark to Brodie. "This is getting worse by the minute. With these two deaths on top of the murdered women, the entire area is going to go into a panic any minute."

"Oh, I don't know," Brodie said dryly. "Neither of these men was anyone important. Their deaths will likely go unnoticed, especially Digger's. We just have to hope the Hildegards don't raise a stink about Jimmy."

"Do you assume, Detective," Edwards asked indignantly, "that I care any less about the unknowns in this city than the biggest mogul?"

"No, of course not," Brodie said.

"He means that he doesn't think the media will go mad the way they do whenever a celebrity dies," Mark said quickly.

"Get out of my face right now, you two," Edwards said. "Get back to the station and get your paperwork filled out. The crime scene unit is on the job, and with luck whoever killed Digger will have left some kind of a clue." He lowered his voice again. "At least they were both human," he muttered. "And a human life is as important as the life of an Other, but at least as far as the autopsies go we won't have to make sure that—"

"No, Lieutenant, think about it," Mark interrupted. "We know all these deaths are connected. Please, try to make sure that Antony Brandt gets assigned the autopsies."

Edwards looked as if he was about to implode, explode—or transform involuntarily into a fully massive, growling, snarling werewolf. "I'll do my best," he finally said.

"And we need a search warrant," Mark said.

"For?"

"Come on, Lieutenant. Jimmy worked for the Hildegard family. I'll bet you cash money that he lived

in that mansion, along with working there. That's
enough to get us a warrant."

"You'd better find something," Edwards warned.

"We will."

"Go. Paperwork."

They left together; by then, the street and the alley
were roped off with crime scene tape, and the foren-
sics units were busy examining the area. The medical examiner on duty wasn't Brandt, but he was a
good man who would make all the notes at the scene,
file an initial report on cause and time of death, and
then see that the bodies were brought to the morgue.

They could still hope that Brandt would get the
autopsies.

"You don't have to deal with the paperwork,"
Mark told Brodie. "You weren't there, really. You
can get back to the house if you want."

"I was first on the scene after you," Brodie said.
"Besides, it will be quicker if I help. Two pencil-
pushers are better than one, and we both need to get
back to the House of the Rising Sun and figure out
where all this puts us."

"Thanks," Mark told him.

Brodie was right; between them, they finished
everything that had to be written up within twenty
minutes. Then they headed for home base.

"Alessande was all right, wasn't she?" Brodie
asked as they drove.

Mark nodded. "It was scary, though." He looked
at Brodie. "Whoever it was took her completely by

surprise. They could have killed her, but they didn't. What do you think that means?"

"Maybe they thought she *was* dead. Or maybe it was the screenwriter. He's infatuated with her. Maybe he's in on what's happening but he couldn't bring himself to kill Alessande. Not that I mean to disturb you in any way," Brodie added, a smile to his voice.

Were his feelings for Alessande so obvious?

Yes, apparently, at least to Brodie. And probably the rest of the group.

"I wish it were that simple," Mark said.

"So you don't think that Greg Swayze is part of the plot?" Brodie confirmed.

Mark thought about the question for a minute. "I think he's just what he seems to be. A screenwriter with a script in production and a crush on a beautiful woman. I don't think he killed Digger."

"Then who?"

"Hopefully we'll know more once we see Declan. He'll be able to tell us if any of the Hildegards or the film crew left when we did, or if they all stayed. If they left, it's telling."

"Even if they didn't leave, the Hildegards are rich. They might have an army out there ready to do their bidding," Brodie reminded him.

"I know. But let's see what we can get. At least we'll be able to search the Hildegard mansion—and maybe we'll luck out and find Regina Johnson," Mark said.

* * *

When they got to the House of the Rising Sun estate, they found that Declan, Sailor and Rhiannon had all come home, and the entire group was gathered around the dining room table of Castle House. Barrie and Mick had their computers out, along with a mass of newspapers and charts.

Mark instantly looked for and found Alessande, who had showered and changed into a casual black knit halter dress that clung to her body in all the right ways. Her hair fell around her face like skeins of molten gold. And her eyes were blue-green and clear when she looked at him and smiled.

"Not even a headache," she assured him.

Brodie took a seat at the table and immediately turned to Declan and Sailor. "The Hildegards and the film people—when did they leave the Snake Pit?"

"The minute Alessande left, Greg Swayze said something to the others at his table and left," Sailor said. "And the Hildegards were right behind him."

"And the film people left a few minutes later," Declan added.

"If the film people hung out even a little while longer, they probably didn't have time to get in on the action," Mark said. "But the Hildegards... And I discounted Swayze earlier, but maybe I shouldn't have."

"Hey, we've come up with some interesting information here," Barrie announced.

"We're all ears," Mark assured her, smiling.

"Okay, Alan Hildegard really does produce pictures for the cable channel Horrific. He's incorporated," Mick Townsend told them. "His parent corporation is called Hildegard Enterprises. But Hildegard has a number of smaller subsidiaries, and one of those is called Dynamic Dough."

"Dynamic Dough?" Alessande repeated.

"Dough—yes, I assume as in money," Barrie said. "Dynamic Dough arranges motion picture financing, and through them Alan Hildegard helps finance a lot of films for both the big studios and the small independents."

"So was he in on the financing when Blue Dove Entertainment decided to do *Death in the Bowery?*" Alessande asked. "I thought that Blue Dove Entertainment was legitimate."

"They are, but you know how when you see a movie it says 'produced by' several times, or they give credit to a few coproducers or executive producers or associate producers? Sometimes you get a producer credit just for providing money. Sometimes you get it because you legitimately did the work to get the money, hire the director, the rest of the crew...putting it all together," Barrie said. "We know that Hildegard couldn't afford to option the script himself but is still associated with the movie. Specifically, we found out that *Death in the Bowery* was going to require a higher budget than Blue Dove Entertainment was willing to risk on its own—despite the fact that our screenwriter is Hollywood's current golden boy. They wanted to go with a fresh face for the heroine, but they wanted to hire a big name, the kind of name that can carry a picture, for the villain. For that kind of star power, they were going to need a big budget—plus they wanted to hire huge talent behind the scenes, like Katrina Manville to do the costumes. And the sets for a historic piece can be almost as pricey as for an action flick where you're blowing cars up every minute."

"So, if he was telling the truth at all," Mark said, "Alan Hildegard was smitten by *Death in the Bowery* and the brilliance of the screenwriter—and the fact that his last movie made a small fortune. Alan was probably thinking that with a real box office draw and some money behind the production, they could rake in the millions. He knows that he can't bankroll something like that on his own and the Horrific channel won't be interested, so he puts a treatment together and goes to someone over at Blue Dove Entertainment, promising that he'll pull together some of the money so they won't have to shoulder the whole risk."

"So Blue Dove gets involved," Sailor went on. "They start the hiring process, bringing in a noted director and casting director—and probably contacting whatever name they want for the villain."

"And," Rhiannon theorized, "Alan now has a semiofficial reason for having and sharing the screenplay. Because he needs tall beautiful blondes to be sacrificed, he uses the screenplay to find them."

"Maybe he makes a point of looking for them at

the House of Illusion because it's so close to the old family studio," Alessande suggested.

"Yes, he meets them, gets the screenplay into their hands and suggests that he can help them with a reading in preparation for their auditions—they just have to meet him at the old studio," Barrie said.

"This is definitely a decent working theory," Mark said. "Who would want to bring back a Hildegard more than another Hildegard? And we know that the priest conducting the ceremony in that tomb was an Other. Someone who could disappear—and a shifter could easily turn into a gnat and vanish."

"Maybe we'll find something concrete tomorrow," Brodie said.

"Tomorrow?" Rhiannon asked. "Where?"

Mark told her, "Because of the Jimmy connection, we're going to get a search warrant."

"Alan Hildegard—whether he killed Digger or not—will know what happened by morning. Won't he expect you to show up?" Alessande asked.

"Maybe. And maybe he'll think himself so high and mighty that nothing will stick. I'm sure he intends to disavow anything to do with Jimmy. The guy was a servant—nothing more," Brodie said. "That's the Hildegard way of thinking."

Mark looked at Alessande. "I'm not sure you should have coffee with Greg Swayze tomorrow. This is getting too dangerous. You've been attacked twice now."

"We're going to have coffee at the Mystic Café," she said. "I'll be fine."

"I'll make sure I'm working," Rhiannon said firmly.

"And Sailor and I can go have a coffee ourselves—not to mention the place is owned by that old werewolf Keeper Hugh Drummond," Declan said. "We'll keep an eye on things, Mark. I promise."

He was pretty sure they were all amused at his overprotectiveness. He supposed it *was* obvious that there was something going on between him and Alessande. Had Charlaine Hildegard figured that out, too? Did it even matter to her, since she was only playing with him anyway?

Why hadn't that gooey-eyed screenwriter figured it out yet? he wondered.

Rhiannon yawned. "Whatever's happening tomorrow, we have to get some sleep tonight."

"Mick and I are out of here," Barrie said, then paused. "We'll leave the computers here, though, and consider Castle House the command center for this…situation."

Rhiannon was already standing, ready to walk back to Pandora's Box.

Brodie turned to Mark. "You coming with?" he asked.

"I thought I'd hang here. Not that I don't have tremendous faith in all the protective spells and things around the property, but I would hate to see Alessande attacked twice in one night."

"Yeah, sure," Brodie said, his lips twitching.

Actually, Mark realized, they all looked at one another, lips twitching. But Alessande didn't protest.

He was staying.

It had been a long day; a painfully long day. But the minute they closed the door of the guest room, Alessande was in his arms with a warmth and need so erotic and evocative that before he knew it, he was stripping off his clothes, desperately eager to feel her naked length against him. His arousal was as acute as if he was sixteen again.

They tangled together, lay together, marveled together, as only new lovers could do. Everything was still unique, and touching her, feeling her touch, created a world of wonder. The caress of her lips running down his naked flesh was pure bliss. Hunger ripped through him in jagged streaks as she teased him with her mouth, her hands. At last they merged in a frenzy of movement, desperate and arousing, urgent, until it felt as if his blood were simmering while his heart hammered and his very being seemed about to explode. After they climaxed, he lay beside her, still feeling a sense of wonder that, even after making love, he couldn't bear to move away from her.

Elven, he reminded himself.

"Vampire," she said softly, offering him a small smile.

And he smiled in return, pulling her closer. "Elven," he said.

"Vampires are known for being the most skilled and fiery lovers," she said.

"And Elven beauty is known to mesmerize and leave those touched by it in awe," he reminded her.

"Oh, come on," she teased, stroking his face. "When we met, you thought I was an absolute bitch."

"You *were* a little rude about having your life saved."

"I did think I had it covered," she said.

He chuckled and stroked her hair. "It was a life well worth saving," he told her, a slight tremor in his voice. "And there was the oddest thing...."

"What?" she asked, rising on one elbow to search his eyes.

"I was dreaming—or daydreaming—about you right before we met."

"Really?" she asked, then bit her lower lip and looked downward for a moment. "That's bizarre. But...confession. I had a dream about you, too. It was wicked and erotic."

He grinned at that, touching her face with wonder. Then he grew serious. What he had envisioned had not been good.

Her eyes widened as she watched him. "Did you dream of something...strange?"

He thought about lying to her. They were still so deep in all this. Then he decided he had to tell her the truth. "The night we saved you at the Hildegard tomb, I had dozed off earlier in the car while we waiting, and I dreamed that I was at a wedding. My wedding. I heard the music, and I saw Brodie…all kinds of people. We were in a church, and I knew that I was insanely in love, ready to get married, looking forward to getting married…and everything was beautiful. There was a red velvet runner up the aisle, leading to the altar. I looked toward the altar and there was a woman lying on it, my bride, and suddenly the runner was blood and the woman had been killed, her throat sliced…."

"And the woman was me?" she asked.

"I thought so, but…who can really tell in a day-dream?"

She let out a soft, tremulous sigh, but her voice was strong. "Before…before I had my very erotic dream about you, I had the same dream you just described."

"What?" He rose up on an elbow, facing her on the bed.

"It was terrifying."

He pulled her back into his arms, trembling as he lay down with her again. "They were just dreams," he said. "But…I think that, being what we are… maybe our dreams mean something. Maybe there was a reason why I saw you right before I met you."

She moved away from him, shaking off his hand when he touched her shoulder. Sleek and beautiful, she rose and walked to the window, moving the drapes aside to look down on the lawn below.

"Maybe it means we're supposed to stay away from one another," she said.

For a moment he froze where he lay.

Maybe she was right.

Yet he couldn't accept that. He stood and walked over to her, setting his hands on her shoulders and pulling her back against him. "I can't believe that," he told her, whispering into her hair. The spun magic of the golden strands teased his lips. He'd never felt anything as intensely as he felt this need to be with her, to know that she lived and breathed in the world.

She turned into his arms, looking up at him. "I *won't* believe it," she said passionately.

He touched a lock of her hair, mesmerized, humbled, as he smoothed it back. "After tonight…"

"Tonight I wasn't ready. I'll never let that happen again, Mark, I swear it. But I can't step aside now. You know I can't. The birthmark that denotes my destiny…the things I've discovered I can do… I am meant to be a Keeper. I can't walk away from that, and you know it. You can't protect me all the time or from everything. You have to see the truth of that, Mark…please."

He smiled. "Brodie still watches out for Rhiannon, and you couldn't convince him not to."

"And *she* watches out for *him,* as well. We all have to have each others' backs, Mark. It's part of being who and what we are."

He wanted to deny her words. He wished that she was sensible and prudent and willing to stay safely hidden away at Castle House until they found the root of the evil plaguing them now.

And then he realized that she wouldn't be the golden spitfire who had so swiftly commandeered his flesh and blood and soul if she were that woman.

He nodded slowly. "But we make a pact. No one goes running off alone for any reason, and we share everything we learn."

"Deal," she told him.

He cupped her head in his hands and tenderly kissed her lips. For a moment something shimmered between them that went far beyond the physical.

She returned the kiss. And then the kiss deepened and was joined by touching. And kissing went from lips to flesh and touching abounded. They stumbled a bit, holding on to one another as they crashed back down upon the bed, their bodies already entwined. They laughed at their own clumsiness, kissed and stroked....

And made love again.

Finally they lay together, fell asleep, and when Mark woke to the hint of daylight that teased through the drapes, he realized that he had not dreamed, he had merely held tightly to a dream all through the night.

Chapter 10

"So, tell me about yourself," Greg Swayze said.

"Tell you what?" Alessande asked him.

"Anything," Swayze breathed, as she sat across the table from him at the Mystic Café.

Rhiannon was working, strumming soft ballads quietly from the dais at the end of the room, while Hugh Drummond, the owner and local werewolf Keeper, kept vigil behind the counter.

Mark and Brodie were at work, but soon after she had arrived and joined Swayze at his table, Barrie and Mick had come in to buy coffee and claim a table nearby, and soon after *they'd* arrived, Declan had also come in with Sailor. They'd made a point of stopping by to say hello to Swayze and Alessande.

"Anything?" Alessande repeated now. "Okay...

my family is originally Norse, but I was born and spent my childhood in Scotland. I love where I'm living now—I'm in the Valley—and I do a lot of gardening when I'm not working. And, frankly, I haven't done much acting. I just love your screenplay so much—that's why I wanted to be involved in the film somehow."

"Thank you. *Death in the Bowery* is a project I've wanted to do for a long, long time. My folks came from New York City, so I've been reading about the history of the city from the time I was a child. I got the idea for the plot from reading about some gruesome murders that occurred at the time and were never solved. But the story's not about going for the gore factor, it's about people. It's about overcoming prejudice. Back then there were people living in mansions the size of a full city block, while there were others eating garbage and living among the rats—desperate just to survive."

"You've painted that picture perfectly with your words," she assured him.

"And you are my ideal Jane Adams," he told her.

"Well, honestly…I think I'd be happier with a smaller role. I love the role, but I really don't have the experience to…" She decided not to push that point at the moment. Instead she decided to see what she could find out about the other members of the production team. "It seems as if everything's falling into place. The director, the costume designer, even the producers…" She smiled. "Imagine having Alan Hildegard involved."

Swayze nodded. "Believe it or not, I was as stunned as the next person when he came on board. He'd read the screenplay and loved it, but he couldn't get backing from the Horrific channel—it's certainly not the kind of thing they do, and they have him pretty well tied up—but they can't control what he does with his own time and money, so the next thing I knew, he had me all set up through Blue Dove and Gnome Entertainment, and if you ask me, I think he's got a stake in one or both of those."

"And you wound up becoming friends with his whole family. That's pretty cool."

"I don't know about being friends, exactly, but they're all supporting the project financially as well, so—all of them have a say in casting, so it's not as if I can make the decision anyway. Honestly, I'm lucky as hell the director is even giving me a say. The biggest problem I'm having right now is that they want a rewrite of the end."

"A rewrite?" Alessande asked.

"They want a twist. They want the villain to win at the end—a statement on truth, Alan says." He shook his head in amazement. "I wasn't stupid when I signed my contract. I kept control over the material. They're still pushing, though. Alan keeps pointing out how many serial killers have gotten away with their crimes over time. And how the victims—so many of them society's disenfranchised, lacking someone to make a fuss when they disappear—have met their ends without being noted."

"Oh," Alessande said.

"Don't worry. They can't change it without my say-so, and so far nothing they've said has convinced me to give it." He looked at her anxiously and put his hand over hers. "Will you still be on board, no matter what?"

"Of course. If the ending *is* rewritten, you'll be the one to rewrite it, correct?"

"Yes—though I like it the way it is." His hand still lingered on hers.

"I'm sure we'll all be on board," she said.

"'We'?"

"Yes. My friend Sailor auditioned, too—remember?" She nodded toward the table where Sailor sat, sipping tea and talking to Declan, who was facing them. It was nice, Alessande thought, how well the group was looking after each other. It was good to feel so safe.

And yet, that thought also made her feel guilty, because *she* should have been there for Regina.

"Right, Sailor Gryffald," Swayze said. "She did a great reading. And she also has the look we're after as well, that kind of blond innocence that can cover a world of strength. And that's the perfect description of Jane Adams. Despite the miserable circumstances of her birth and the squalor in which she's been raised, she believes in the goodness of people. But, she's not stupid. She knows that evil is out there—she's seen it. Yes, Sailor would do very well in the role. Except, of course...there's you."

There's me—because, for some reason, you're obsessed with me, Alessande thought.

"You're both going to be getting callbacks," he went on.

"That's great," she said. "Thank you."

She didn't know how to end the conversation and leave, but she definitely thought it was time to go. After speaking with him, she was pretty sure he was entirely innocent. There was a way to make sure, of course. She was worried, though, about leading him on or appearing flirtatious.

Still, it had to be done.

She smiled and stared directly into his eyes, and concentrated on listening to the words that were in his mind rather than those he spoke.

Mark and Brodie's first stop was the hospital, where they were able to see Chelsea Rose.

She was weak and looked as frail as the delicate rose petal her name invoked as she lay in her hospital bed.

She offered a tiny smile when she saw them. "You're the detectives who saved my life," she said. "Thank you."

"We're glad to see you awake and still here with us," Brodie told her.

"Thank you," she said.

It disturbed Mark to realize just how blonde and

blue-eyed she was. He knew instantly that she wasn't Elven—but with her looks, she could have been. And that made him worry more about Alessande.

But Alessande was in a public place and surrounded by friends. He had to trust in them to keep her safe. He knew that, but it didn't make it any easier.

"Chelsea, can you tell us anything that might help us find the people selling the drug that nearly killed you?" Mark asked her.

She frowned. "I saw the newspaper today. It sounds like the man who was behind it is dead. James someone—a butler. I didn't even know people still had butlers. And that the guy who actually sold us the pill was killed, too."

"That's the problem, Chelsea," Mark said. "Digger—the dealer—was killed *after* James Laughton was already dead. That means that someone else is still out there. And that someone is the person in charge. James wasn't in charge. He was working for someone else, just like Digger was, and Digger wasn't about to fall on his sword."

Her mind was obviously still working slowly. "He had a sword?" she asked.

Brodie and Mark exchanged a stunned glance, then Brodie took the question. "That's just an expression, Chelsea. It means someone is either so afraid of or so loyal to his boss that he's willing to die rather than risk a police interrogation and possibly give something away."

"Oh!" she said, blushing.

Mark took the chair at her bedside and glanced out to the hallway. The police guard was in his chair, reading the paper. There were no nurses or doctors in sight.

"Chelsea, look at me, please," Mark said. He stared at her intently. "Just relax and think about everything you did that night. Try to picture the street when you two ran into Digger. Tell me everything you saw."

She stared back at him. She didn't blink.

"Easy…just let your mind go back," he said.

"We wanted a high, something fun. I remember telling Terry that night that L.A. can be so random. Like, you have the Snake Pit, but you turn a few corners and it's all crack houses. He said that was great for us, because we could score but still be kind of safe. I didn't feel very safe, though, and I just wanted to go back, but by then we were lost. We saw a few really grungy people, but we didn't even speak to them, but then that man—Digger—came up to us. He told us he could get us to a safer street. And then he asked if we were looking to get high and said he had just what we wanted, and offered us that pill. He said only one of us should take it, because whoever took it would get really, well, horny, so the other one needed to be more with it. Terry… he always wants to have sex, like…day and night… and I work and sometimes I'm tired and not so into it. So *I* took the pill…."

She paused; her eyes never left Mark's, but something seemed to strike her from deep in her memory. "I remember the sound," she said.

"What sound?" Mark asked.

"Whoosh," she said.

"Whoosh?" he prodded.

"Yes, a whoosh. I thought it was weird, because I didn't see any birds, but it sounded like…something flying by. Like wings. I said something about it, but Terry didn't hear it. I had taken the pill by then, though, so maybe that was it."

"And then?" Mark pressed.

"Then…I woke up here, in the hospital."

It was clearly all he was going to get. Mark made a point of blinking to release her from his hold. "Thank you, Chelsea."

"Is Terry okay?" she asked anxiously.

"He's fine," Mark assured her.

"Can I see him?" she asked.

"Sure, we'll make it happen," Brodie said. "We'll see what we can do, say, later this afternoon or tonight."

She blinked and frowned, confused. "How odd," she said.

"What's that?" Mark asked.

"I hadn't remembered that until you asked me, but it felt like there were birds all around in the sky, but I couldn't see them. I actually looked—and there were no birds."

"Thank you, Chelsea," Mark said. "You've been very helpful."

They left the hospital. It was still early, but Mark was anxious. "I'd asked earlier for a search warrant for the Hildegard house. Let's pick that up and then head over there."

"We have to run by the station and coordinate," Brodie reminded him.

"Why? They could meet us—"

"Edwards left a message on my cell while we were in with Chelsea. He wants to talk to us," Brodie said.

Mark groaned. "Something isn't right, then. Let's get moving. The more time that passes, the more time the Hildegards have to hide whatever they've been up to."

Alessande sat in the backseat wedged between Sailor and Barrie.

"So...I don't understand exactly what happened," Declan said from behind the wheel. "You read his mind, he didn't look away, but you didn't get anything."

"I got some things," she said. "Just nothing exactly...useful. Mainly, he was wondering what his next move should be to get me into bed."

"At least he wasn't thinking about killing you," Sailor said.

"Maybe he *is* just a pawn in the big game," Barrie suggested.

"I don't know. All I got was what was foremost

in his brain. Oh, Sailor—he knows you're the better actress, but he also knows that you're with Declan and he still believes he's got a shot with me. If the movie does happen—"

Sailor laughed. "I'm sure there are still other contenders for the role, and anyway, last time I thought I'd get a break, it turned out I was dealing with a bunch of criminals and killers—just like might be happening now. Not to mention that my agent turned out to...well, let's not go back there. Alessande, please don't worry. I have faith in myself. I love acting, and I *will* get my breakout part. So let's use his interest in you until we get what we need, okay?"

"I just don't know if we *will* get what we need," Alessande said. "If the real players are Others, they know how to hide their thoughts—how to avoid an Elven's eyes...." She let her voice trail off and hesitated. "I think we're going to have to consider shifting—even if our enemies are actual shapeshifters."

"Possibly," Declan said, glancing at Mick. "Possibly. But shifting's dangerous. It takes a lot out of you—and you could wind up in a precarious situation after shifting. There's got to be a better way."

"Mark and Brodie are getting a search warrant. I'm sure they'll find out something today," Barrie said with confidence.

"And don't forget Merlin," Alessande said. "The day we figured out I'm in line to be a Keeper, Merlin was telling me about Sebastian. We need to talk to Merlin again—get him to tell us everything he possibly can."

"Great idea—maybe Merlin can steer us in a better direction," Barrie said.

When they reached the estate of the House of the Rising Sun, Wizard greeted them enthusiastically in the yard. He preferred watching over the house from outside, but when they went inside, he followed them. He and Jonquil began racing through the living room. Barrie told the two massive dogs to behave or take it out to the yard. Both whined and looked at the door, and she let them back out.

"I'll make tea," Barrie said.

"Yes, of course, tea—we drink tea a lot, don't we?" Declan asked.

"Tea grows from the earth and brings strength," Alessande said.

"So do carrots," Declan said.

Alessande laughed. "Ask any Brit or Irishman—they'll tell you to have a cup of tea. Besides, its known for its medicinal powers."

"I think I'll have a beer," Mick said, heading to the refrigerator. "Cool and refreshing—add a hot dog and it's good old-fashioned American medicine." He looked around at the empty air. "Merlin? You here, Merlin? We need you."

There was no response.

"I'll head over to Pandora's Box, see if he's there," Declan said.

"I'll try Gwydion's Cave," Mick said.

"Good idea. He likes to hang out at my place," Barrie said. "I get several papers, and he loves to read them. He's so proud that he can turn the pages."

"Next thing you know, we'll be getting him his own e-reader. He'll have a heyday once he masters it," Alessande said.

"That's a great idea," Barrie said. "He's always so helpful. Providing him with a new challenge would be a nice thank-you."

She left to brew the tea—no matter that they had just left a coffee shop—and Mick and Declan went off to look for Merlin. In a few minutes they were back, with the ghostly magician in tow. Everyone adjourned to the dining room with their tea, or beer, and Merlin sat at the head of the table.

"I'm not sure what else I can tell you," he said, addressing the group. "As I said, I remember Sebastian. He entertained at the House of Illusion often enough. He liked to bill himself as Sebastian the Magnificent or the Dark Enchanter—he loved to saw people in half and that kind of thing. He practiced his scripts—not just his illusions. He told the audience that 'the lords of the shadows' listened to him. He was very dramatic, and audiences loved him. In fact, sometimes his illusions weren't all that good, but people didn't care, because they enjoyed listening to him—they liked his showmanship. He told me once that I should honor him as a god, and then he could see to it that I lived forever. Thankfully, I never fell for his malarkey."

They were all silent. Merlin might not have lived forever, but he had figured out how to stay around in his own way.

"Maybe those are key words," Alessande said thoughtfully. "'Lords of the shadows' and 'Dark Enchanter.' Maybe we could find something about what he was up to in old newspaper stories," she said, looking over at Barrie and Mick.

They seemed to be considering it. "To go back that far…" Barrie murmured.

"We'll need to go to the office and see what we can find," Mick said. "But we can do that now."

"Let me see…." Merlin said thoughtfully. "Oh, yes! He claimed that he was a high priest of the cult of…something or other."

"Something or other?" Alessande pressed.

"Something…pagan," Merlin said. "Ah! I remember. He said he was a high priest in the Cult of Tyr. But I can't remember just who—"

"Laptop!" Barrie said, rushing off to grab Sailor's.

"Tyr is a Norse god," Alessande said. "He's the god of combat, among other things. In English, the day of the week Tuesday comes from his name." They all stared at her. She shrugged. "I was born in Scotland, but my parents were Norse. I heard all the stories and legends when I was very young. Tyr is also the god of victory and triumph."

"Victory and triumph—over death?" Sailor asked.

Barrie had found a website on the Norse gods and spoke up. "Alessande is right."

"But you could be on to something," Mick pointed out to Sailor. "Victory—triumph. Sebastian saw himself as a priest, a warrior—a ruler. Someone to have victory over death."

Barrie had started typing again. "You won't believe what I just found! This is a site on the history of L.A., and there's a picture of Sebastian Hildegard here." She stared at them in disbelief. "He was a suspect in the murder of a young woman found in a vacant lot off Sunset just weeks before his own death." She hesitated, reading quickly, then looked at them again. "Her throat had been slit. He was never charged, and his name never hit the media, but he was considered a person of interest, and he was interviewed."

"Merlin, did you know about this?" Alessande asked.

Merlin shook his head. "The most scandalous murder of my day was the Black Dahlia," he said. "I don't remember hearing anything about this case."

"It was never solved," Barrie said, still reading.

"Why would he have been a suspect? Sunset is long and well traveled—why would a body discovered there arouse suspicion about Hildegard?" Alessande asked.

Barrie gasped softly. "Because of the cement the cops found on her."

"Cement? What are you talking about?" Alessande asked.

"The Hildegard tomb was just being built when

the girl was found," Barrie said. "They found cement dust on her that looked like the same cement being used to build the tomb."

"What did Hildegard die of?" Mick asked, leaning over Barrie.

"Cancer," Merlin said. "He'd been treated for it for a while. Unusual for a shifter, but it can be just as fatal as for anyone else."

"So he knew he was dying," Alessande said. "And he was in that cult, so...maybe he killed her so her blood could be used for some kind of sacrament when he was laid in his tomb. And maybe the people who want him back revived the cult, or maybe founded a version of their own, knew that somehow."

"Or maybe they were familiar with the family tales," Sailor said thoughtfully.

"Is there a description of the victim in the article?" Alessande asked Barrie.

"Not here...let me try searching the name...." She typed for a moment and then started reading aloud to them. "'Aspiring actress Belinda Bevin was twenty-six, five-eight, blue-eyed and blonde. Her friends described her as *magically beautiful*.'"

"Elven," they all said in unison.

Alessande considered everything for a moment. "Neither of the recent victims was Elven. And we have no way of knowing for sure if this victim was, either. Let's say she was, though, and that she was killed because her blood was important for Sebastian's burial, maybe to ensure that he'd be able to come back someday. And now they need Elven blood to accomplish that return." She looked around at the others to see what they thought of her theory.

Sailor gasped softly. "Elven don't get cancer," she said.

"Or," Declan suggested, "maybe Elven blood was chosen because Elven have magic in them, but they're not as deadly as, say, a vampire or a werewolf. And, in mythology, vampires and werewolves are associated with darkness and death, while Elven are associated with light, life and healing."

"Whatever the reason," Alessande said, "I believe that whoever wants to raise Sebastian from the dead conducted a few 'trial runs' using non-Elven women just to make sure they could get through the ceremony without making a mistake. That's why the police received the anonymous tip to be at the Hildegard tomb the other night. The cult had taken a woman they knew was Elven and planned to conduct the ritual for real. For publicity."

"That all makes sense—except for one thing," Barrie said.

"What's that?" Mick asked.

"They were already holding an Elven. Regina Johnson. Why didn't the call come sooner?" Barrie asked.

"I don't know, but they still have Regina," Sailor said.

"And that means the whole thing is still set to go with an Elven sacrifice," Alessande said. "We just have to stop them before they can complete the next ceremony. The ringleaders are probably lying low now because they made such a lucky escape last time."

"While we wait for them to make their next move, we need to find out more about this Cult of Tyr and what Sebastian was up to before he died," Sailor said.

Declan slammed his hand down on the table. "No," he said. "What we need to do is dig up the body of Sebastian Hildegard and burn it to ash— that will stop whatever is going on."

"But it won't help us find Regina," Alessande said. "They're holding her—and if we destroy their chance of raising Sebastian, they'll kill her. They've already killed twice, after all." She grew thoughtful for a moment, then said, "There *is* a way...."

"And that is?" Sailor asked.

"We dig up Sebastian without anyone knowing."

Chapter 11

"I don't know what to tell you. This is all we could get," Bryce Edwards said irritably.

Mark stared at him. "Lieutenant, this won't give us anything. We needed a warrant for the whole house. All we're going to do is piss off Alan Hildegard when we come in with something like this."

"Lieutenant," Brodie said. "Doesn't the D.A. want this thing solved?" He looked around the station and lowered his voice. "We have to get an Other judge who'll give us a better warrant."

"Judge Varlet is a vampire," Edwards said softly. "He says he still has to follow the letter of the law, and that warrant is good for the butler's personal space and the kitchen. That's all they can do. So far, we don't have an iota of evidence that suggests that

Alan Hildegard—or Brigitte or Charlaine—might be involved with the drug business in any way."

"We caught people in the Hildegard tomb—" Mark began.

"And the leaders escaped or disappeared. We didn't end up with a single thing on the people you *did* bring in—every story they gave us checked out. They were just dumb minions roped in to fill some kind of quorum. You have nothing that implicates any member of the Hildegard family," Edwards said. "You both know the law."

"Yeah, but the problem is, this isn't going to fall into the regular scope of the law," Mark said.

Edwards leaned closer, speaking very softly. "Then you two need to work outside the law. But whatever you do, don't get caught. I suggest, however, that you *do* serve this warrant. I can send officers with you. Make sure you have Alan Hildegard, his sister and his cousin believing that you're convinced only the butler had anything to do with the drug and probably the murder, that he had heard the family stories about Sebastian and was probably trying to curry favor with the family by bringing their patriarch back."

"Better than nothing," Brodie told Mark.

"I guess," Mark said. "Still, a butler has full run of the house. Couldn't we have used that angle?"

"I got what I could get. Now you two use what *you* have and get this done," Edwards told them.

A few minutes later, as the detectives left the station, Brodie asked quietly, "Did he just tell us to use whatever Other powers we have to cut through this?"

"Sounded like it to me," Mark said, then he made a call to alert the team that Edwards had assigned to them. They arrived at the mansion to be met by six officers and forensic specialists.

Alan Hildegard answered the door himself.

Of course; he didn't have a butler any longer.

"I've been expecting you," Alan said. "Come on through—I'll show you to Jimmy's apartment."

The bastard knew what their warrant contained!

Of course. He wasn't stupid.

Both Brigitte and Charlaine were there, as well. Brigitte watched them silently as they entered; Charlaine smiled at Mark. "Detective, what a pleasure to see you, again. Of course, the circumstances are terrible—we're just shocked about Jimmy, of course. He was a wonderful butler. But I suppose that watching us…seeing this house, the family money…made him long to make some real money of his own. Sadly, he decided to do it by selling drugs. I'm horrified, just horrified. The young people who might have been hurt…it's just terrible."

"Unfortunately, Jimmy wasn't working on his own, Charlaine," Mark said, contravening the lieutenant's suggestion and not caring.

"What makes you think that?" Alan asked, walking up behind him.

"For one thing, he killed himself rather than be arrested," Mark said.

Alan shrugged. "I'd kill myself, too, before I'd let myself be confined."

"Don't be silly," Charlaine said. "You'd never be confined." She dropped her voice so that only Mark and Brodie could hear her next words. "You'd turn yourself into a bee or a wasp and fly right out of prison. But, that *is* a good point. I think a lot of people would prefer death to being locked away."

"Well, there's another reason—I'm sure you read in the papers that Jimmy was working with a man who went by the street name Digger. Digger was murdered," Mark said.

"Jimmy murdered this…Digger before he died?" Brigitte asked.

"No."

"How do you know?" Alan asked.

"Because Digger was killed after Jimmy was already dead," Mark said.

"Interesting. The papers didn't say who was killed when. I'd rather assumed Jimmy had murdered his cohort, then killed himself," Alan said. "Anyway, come through this way, will you? Jimmy had his own apartment. It's the entire attic, actually. Take your time, and if there's anything we can do to help you…"

"Actually, there is," Mark said. "Laughton was your butler. He had the run of the house. With your permission, we can search everywhere."

"My, my! How industrious," Charlaine said.

"You're more than welcome to search my suite. I'll go along to help in any way I can."

"I agree," Brigitte added. "Search anywhere you like."

"Alan?" Brodie asked.

"Go for it," Alan told him. "We were appalled to discover that a member of our household was involved in this ridiculous cult that's grown up around our great-grandfather, not to mention *murder*. Search anywhere you like."

"We're going to need a bigger crew," Brodie murmured to Mark. His tone was one of definite surprise.

"I'll call it in," Mark said, looking at Alan. *Had they been wrong about all this?*

He studied the three members of the Hildegard family. Alan returned his regard with what appeared to be sincerity. Brigitte stood quietly by her brother.

Charlaine, though... Charlaine was smiling just like the cat that had eaten the canary.

He realized that they could search all they wanted, but they wouldn't find anything. No, actually, they would.

They would find it in Jimmy's apartment—right where it had already been planted.

But they needed to go through the motions.

"Thank you," he told them. "Thing is, he might have put anything anywhere—intending for you to be blamed." If they wanted to play a game of lies, he and Brodie could play it just as well.

"I hadn't thought of that," Alan said. "Still, search

wherever you want to, Detectives. We'll be in the parlor, if you need anything."

"And, of course, though we're down a butler, I do know how to brew tea, so let me know if any of your people would like a bit of refreshment," Brigitte offered.

"That's kind of you," Mark said. He nodded to Brodie to stay with the family while he put through the call to the lieutenant.

"Detective," Charlaine said, "why don't you join me—I'll help you search my quarters first."

"Sure, I'll get some officers," he said.

He was startled when she brushed past him and tripped. When he bent to help her, she whispered to him, "I need to see you alone."

Curious, Mark followed her up the stairs to her second-floor suite.

Rhiannon returned to the house while the others were making plans. When she heard what they'd come up with, she said incredulously, "So we're going to break into the Hildegard tomb, somehow remove Sebastian from his sarcophagus and burn him to ash. And by some miracle no one is going to notice this?"

"Well, we're going to need Mark's and Brodie's help," Alessande said.

"Two cops—great. There go their careers if we're caught," Rhiannon said.

"Have you got a better plan?" Barrie asked her.

Rhiannon considered it. "No," she admitted. "So tell me—how are we going to execute this plan, and, once it's accomplished, how do we find Regina?"

"We've got to keep it entirely secret—that's the only way to keep Regina safe," Alessande said. "We need to send the men into the tomb, so you, Sailor, Barrie and I will have to stay outside and stand watch."

"I'll be something very small—like a caterpillar. I'm good at caterpillars," Barrie said. "That way, if there *is* trouble, I can get into the tomb unseen and warn the guys to get out. It's risky, but it's a risk I think we need to take, given everything we've found out."

"We'll all need to be prepared to step forward and mesmerize anyone who stumbles on us," Alessande told Rhiannon and Sailor. "Between us, we should be able to handle who- and whatever comes our way."

"Unless it's the entire Cult of Tyr," Sailor said.

Rhiannon groaned softly. "Do Brodie and Mark know about this plan yet?"

"No," Alessande said. "And I think we'd better wait and tell them in person, don't you?"

In answer, Rhiannon only groaned again.

As soon as they reached her room, Charlaine dropped the coquettish-flirt act. She closed the door behind her. "I don't know what's going on," she swore. "But it's not going on in our family. Alan isn't lying to you—he doesn't want Sebastian coming back from the dead. He likes being head of the family. Brigitte...Brigitte follows Alan's lead, because she doesn't like doing any actual work. As long as Alan keeps everything going, she's a happy camper. I have to admit, I'm not fond of work myself. I *am* fond of dancing at the Snake Pit, enjoying lunch at the Beverley Hills Hotel and shopping on Rodeo Drive. I like this house, Mark. I like living big and rich in Hollywood."

"In that case, can you tell me how James Laughton, your butler and a human being, wound up dealing Transymil—street name XF—a drug previously confined to the Otherworld?"

"I don't know—I swear, I don't know. I never heard anything about any of this until those women were found dead. And then you and your partner swooped into the family tomb and arrested a bunch of people I'd never even heard of, much less met. Honestly—I'm telling you the truth. And I'm begging you to believe me, because you have to find who's *really* out there killing, because—"

She broke off and stared at him—an entirely different woman from the one who had behaved as if she couldn't wait to jump his bones.

"Because of what?"

She inhaled. "Because I believe that Sebastian *can* be brought back from the grave—and because he shouldn't be." She shuddered. "I've studied the journals he left, and...I know that he murdered a woman before he died. I know that he murdered her with his own hands, that he drank a pint of her blood and covered his body with another pint. And I know that it will take the murder—the sacrifice—of another woman to bring him back to life."

"A blue-eyed blonde?"

She hesitated again. She straightened. "You're not going to want any of your human forensic specialists to find this," she said. As she spoke, she walked over to the medieval-style headboard of her bed and twisted one of the carved rosettes.

He heard a soft whir and watched as one of the walls—at exactly the point where the wallpaper and paneling met, a place he doubted their best experts would have discovered—opened to reveal shelves filled with books, many of them ancient.

Charlaine selected one and handed it to him. "It's Sebastian's diary," she said. "It chronicles his discovery that he had cancer, his desperate search for a cure…and how he stumbled upon a book of the ancients and the Cult of Tyr."

"Tyr?" Mark said, frowning.

"In Norse mythology he was one of the strongest of the gods. He sacrificed his hand to the wolf Fenrir in order to see him bound and secured so he could do no more harm. But the key point about his modern followers is that they believed they could attain eternal life through sacrifice to him. Listen to me, Mark," she said earnestly. "Do I know for a fact that Sebastian can come back? No. But I believe that *he* believed it. And he dabbled in devil worship,

as well. But I still don't believe that either Alan or
Brigitte is involved. All I know is that this started
three months ago when Greg Swayze brought that
screenplay to Alan. I just don't know *why,* or what
the connection is."

"Then we need to let the experts see what James
Laughton left behind, and you and I need to have a
long talk with Alan," Mark told her.

They had assembled what they were going to
need. Everyone had changed into black clothing, and
they were ready with kerosene, flashlights, crowbars,
chisels and hammers. And matches.

Alessande was making a final check of their supplies when the door to Castle House opened, and
Brodie and Mark walked in.

"What are you doing?" Mark asked.

Alessande looked at him and took a deep breath.
"We're going to break into the Hildegard tomb,"
she told him, then rushed ahead with the rest of her
speech before he had a chance to object. "We're
going to steal Sebastian Hildegard's body and burn
it. Declan shifted and flew over to run reconnais-
sance and make sure the coast is clear."

Mark walked over to her, smiling, and tenderly
touched her cheek. "We're not going to break into
the Hildegard tomb."

"We are. We have to. And *you* have to hear what
we've found out. When Sebastian was dying, he
founded a mystical cult dedicated to the Norse god

Tyr because he thought he'd found a way to cheat the cancer that was killing him and come back from the dead. Even though he was never charged, it looks like he murdered a woman so he could use her blood in the ritual he'd dreamed up. We believe she was—"

"Elven," Mark said.

Frowning, Alessande nodded. "Yes, and we think the two women killed so far were for practice, so they could be sure they had the ritual down pat."

"Or maybe the resurrection calls for two human sacrifices before the final sacrifice, which has to be an Elven," Mark said.

"That's possible, too. At any rate, it's clear that Sebastian was evil and it would be bad news if he came back to life, so if we get rid of his body, we eliminate that threat. But we have to do it in secret because they're still holding Regina, and we need them to keep her alive until we can rescue her. If they know Sebastian's body has been destroyed, they'll kill her, and we want them to plan another attempt to resurrect him. So, I know this is hard with you and Brodie being cops—"

Brodie broke in then. "Mark's right. We're not going to break into the tomb."

"But we have to!" Alessande insisted.

"No, we don't," Mark said.

He stepped aside, and she saw that he was not alone. Charlaine Hildegard was standing in the hallway of Castle House right behind Mark and Brodie.

Charlaine smiled at her. "We have an order of exhumation," she explained quietly. "My cousin Alan has signed it as legal next of kin. We're still going in secret, and it will take some effort to keep anyone from finding out what we've done, but at least no one has to break in."

"Oh," Alessande said.

She turned and realized that the others were standing behind her, staring at Mark, Brodie and Charlaine in as much shock as she was.

Distrust was heavy in the air.

"Whether you want to believe me or not," Charlaine said, "I'm facilitating something you want to happen. We'll still be entering in darkness to keep anyone from knowing what we're doing."

"But *you'll* know, won't you?" Alessande said.

"I don't know what to say or do to make you believe I'm on your side," Charlaine said.

"I do," Mark said, and reached into his jacket pocket to produce a book. "Sebastian's diary, which Charlaine gave me of her own free will. It may even tell us a way to end this."

"Darkness has fallen," Brodie said. "We need to get going."

Alessande had to admit, Charlaine had made a complete turnaround. She wasn't smiling, flirting or touching anyone—especially Mark. Still…

They took two cars. Declan had provided the van he used for hauling things to and from the Snake Pit—perfect for taking the body from the cemetery.

For their second vehicle they used Mick's new car, a Honda Odyssey that could seat eight.

The cemetery was empty. A large pair of bolt cutters took care of the lock on the gate, and they kept the headlights off as they drove up to the tomb to avoid being seen.

Charlaine had the keys to the tomb—which made Alessande wonder how the crowd had gotten in the night she had nearly been sacrificed. But no sooner had she decided to wait on that question until they'd finished for the night than Charlaine said, "Jimmy must have gotten hold of the keys that night—it would have been easy enough for him. They're kept on a hook by the kitchen door." She paused. "Participating in the cult would have given him access to Others and the drug, in whatever order it occurred." She looked directly at Alessande. "And not through the Hildegards."

So much for that bit of intrigue.

The women stood guard outside and watched through the iron gate serving as a door while the men went in. Brodie and Mark worked at chiseling off the massive slab of marble with the effigy of Sebastian, and finally they succeeded then lifted the weighty lid.

"Careful," Brodie cautioned.

"Absolutely," Mark agreed. "If we smash it to smithereens, this whole mission is doomed."

While they struggled to set it down, Mick and Declan used the crowbar on the old coffin lid, which gave easily in comparison.

A puff of fetid air escaped, and then they were looking at the remains of Sebastian Hildegard.

Charlaine walked over and gazed into the casket. "Interesting. I would have thought he'd be perfectly preserved."

Abandoning the door, Alessande and the three cousins joined her in staring at the remains.

Sebastian Hildegard's skin had turned dark and leathery, and he looked almost mummified.

Alessande glanced from the corpse to the effigy. It was impossible to tell if they were one and the same.

"The suit…the suit is definitely custom-tailored—just as all his were," Charlaine said.

"How do we know it's really him?" Alessande asked suspiciously.

Brodie and Mark had set down the massive slab of marble and came over to see the corpse, as well.

"We've come this far. Let's get him into the van," Mark said.

Alessande still didn't feel right about things. But she supposed that because his followers all thought he could come back to life, she—like Charlaine—had thought he would be perfectly preserved, as if he'd been laid to rest days ago, instead of decades.

She backed away as Mark leaned forward and lifted the corpse. It was stiff. Dust fell as he shifted the body, and an odor of decay swept through the tomb.

Mark handed the body off to Declan, who took it

outside. Alessande and the Gryffalds closed the coffin, and then Mark and Brodie lifted the giant marble slab back into place.

When they were done, Rhiannon surveyed the area. "We've done it. It looks as if no one has been here."

"Then let's go. We're taking him to the Borden Mortuary," Mark said. "We've got another—" he paused, looking at his watch "—five hours, then people will start arriving for work."

"The Borden Mortuary?" Alessande asked.

"It's owned by Hugh Drummond's family," Mark explained quickly.

"The werewolf who owns the Mystic Café," Rhiannon said.

"I know, I know," Alessande said. "Let's just get there."

Charlaine saw to it that the mausoleum was locked and secure, and then they piled into the cars. Alessande rode with Declan, Sailor, Mark and the corpse. She tried not to look at it. Tried not to imagine that it was going to come to life behind her, reach over the seat and place dead, decaying fingers around her throat.

The corpse didn't move.

They reached the mortuary and pulled around back. Declan had barely parked before he'd exited the van and rushed around to open the rear doors to reach for the corpse. Brodie, who had the keys to the business, opened the entrance that led directly into the morticians' prep room. By then the others had arrived and Mick hurried forward to the massive incinerator.

Alessande tried not to look around, but she couldn't help sneaking a peek.

An elderly woman, freshly made-up, waiting only for her hair to be completed, lay on one of the preparation tables. Another held an older man.

A third held the body of a young male who had apparently been killed in a terrible accident; the morticians were working to restore his face. This being Hollywood, they knew the secrets of special effects makeup and had it almost resembling what it may have been.

She felt chilled. With Others owning the place, anyone could work here.

Including shapeshifters.

She kept imagining that one of the corpses would spring from its preparation table and attack them. Maybe all three.

The rest of their group didn't seem to be bothered by any such thoughts. The crematory temperature was raised, and the body of Sebastian Hildegard was set on the slide and sent into the fire.

The door was closed and locked. The flames burned high.

"It's hot enough, right?" Barrie asked.

Mark checked the gauge. "Optimum," he said. "Eighteen-hundred degrees."

"How long?" Alessande heard herself ask. She was grateful that her voice didn't quiver.

"Two and a half hours," Brodie answered. "A long

time to sit here among the dead. A few of us could head on out."

"If the opportunity's up for grabs," Rhiannon said, "I've been working long hours all over town and I'd love to get home."

"I should get back, too," Charlaine said. "I would just as soon not be spotted coming home in the wee hours by one of the household staff."

Declan said, "All right, I'll take the van and bring Rhiannon, Charlaine and whoever else home."

"I'll stay. I need to see this through," Mark said.

Alessande wanted to scream. If Mark was staying, she felt that she should stay, too. She had walked into this whole thing with so much courage, and yet here in the mortuary, where people worked daily, where death was accepted, she was afraid.

But something about the whole night had seemed off to her.

Charlaine Hildegard suddenly becoming one of them?

Or the condition of the corpse?

"I'll stay with Mark. Everyone else can go home and get some sleep," Alessande heard herself say. "Mark and I will be fine."

Everyone thanked her, and when they were gone, she sat at one of the morticians' desks and tried to smile at Mark. "So, how did it go at the Hildegard mansion? Did you find anything interesting besides the diary?"

"Laughton lived in the attic suite, and it was full of evidence," Mark told her. "A box of the pills, and a veritable forest of carefully tended Transymil plants. He had lights set up...heaters, water gauges, you name it. Everything."

"And you believe he was behind everything?"

"Not on your life." He smiled and walked over to her. "I've never been the least bit attracted to Charlaine, you know. But she did give me the diary. *And* she made it easier for us to accomplish what we have tonight."

"I just wish I knew for sure that that's really Sebastian Hildegard's corpse burning in there," she said. "Anyway, there's a coffee machine. Do you want some?"

"Sure. We do have a long wait."

While the coffee finished brewing, she turned to look around the room again. The far end—with the giant incinerator—seemed to glow red. The walls were full of open shelving holding makeup, wigs and all kinds of paraphernalia for making the dead look as if they were still alive. The morticians had been using some kind of putty on the face of the accident victim. It seemed odd that even in a mortuary, everything was so very Hollywood. Here, just as on the silver screen, the entire focus was on effects. Special effects. Effects to make it look as if the dead were alive, as if they were only sleeping, so that their loved ones could feel comforted that they truly were resting in peace.

The minute the coffee was ready, she poured two cups and brought one over to Mark.

He smiled at her and pointed to the rear of the incinerator. "There's a scoop there, so we can collect the ashes and head to the ocean. I think we need to make sure they're well and truly scattered."

"It's a plan," Alessande said. She sat next to him and sipped her coffee. The elderly man, the elderly woman and the young accident victim lay on their tables without moving.

His fingers curled around hers and she looked over at him. She saw so much in his amber eyes, fire and, more importantly, tenderness.

"You shouldn't have stayed. I would have been all right alone," he told her.

She smiled and kissed the hand that held hers. "No. And I'm fine. I'm with you. It's just…"

"Just what?"

"I don't know. Something about tonight just doesn't feel right."

He leaned back and looked thoughtful.

"You feel it, too!"

"We'll just wait for the ashes, then scatter them and go home. Or to Castle House, as the case is for now. And then…a really long, hot shower."

"I'm willing to share the guest bath," she said, smiling, then leaned against his shoulder to wait.

Eventually the oven finished doing its job. Mark found one of the boxes where ashes were kept when the family hadn't decided on an urn yet. She followed his directions, helping him as they scooped the old magician's remains into the box.

Mark didn't seem to worry about the niceties of

the situation. Now and then they came upon a fragment of bone and he just smashed it with the scoop.

Soon they were ready to go.

"The coffee area…back the way it was?" he asked.

She looked around, then nodded. He picked up the box and they headed out. Just as they were about to close and lock the door, Alessande felt a prickle of apprehension.

She heard something.

She hesitated and looked back into the room. The elderly man lay just as he had been.

She stared at the accident victim.

Did he twitch?

No, it was her imagination.

"Alessande?" Mark said.

"I'm coming. I'm—"

She broke off. It wasn't the accident victim who had moved.

It was the elderly woman. The one who looked like the kind of grandma who made chocolate chip cookies and served them to her beloved grandchildren along with ice-cold milk.

The woman sprang up and came at them, her face contorting and twisting.

And then she morphed completely, becoming a massive tiger and lunging toward them with a deafening growl and the strength of pure muscled feline power.

Chapter 12

Mark realized he should have seen it coming. No matter what, he knew it was prudent to be suspicious at all times.

Actually, being suspicious was his nature.

But he had looked at all the corpses when they had entered and had checked for movement. Now he berated himself for also, and unintentionally, thinking instinctively, distrusting the young man who, even with half his face ripped off, had looked the most powerful.

He'd never suspected the grandmotherly old woman.

Damn shapeshifters. Of course it made sense to choose a seemingly innocuous form.

He slammed the door behind them, but it nearly came off its hinges as the creature slammed against it.

He shoved the box of ashes into Alessande's hands and shouted, "Get in the car!"

"No! You might need me."

"We *need* the ashes," he said, leaning with all his might against the door.

She nodded and hurried to the minivan, throwing open the door.

Suddenly he felt the weight against the door ease. He looked down, afraid the shapeshifter had decided to become something small and escape underneath the door.

He heard glass crashing and turned. The massive beast had vaulted through one of the rear windows and was moving rapidly in his direction.

Mark instantly morphed into a bat, and then his attacker shifted into the form it had used the first time he had seen it: a giant bird of prey.

He swooped and soared, trying to get above it so he could plummet down and get it by the neck. Once his bite was secure he could sink his fangs into it and start to drain it, forcing it to lose strength and careen toward earth.

But as if it knew his intent, the shapeshifter flew higher, staying above him.

"Hey!" he heard Alessande shouting. And then, before his eyes, swiftly and easily, she transformed. She became a bird, a peregrine falcon, and soared into the sky to join the battle.

The giant hawk turned, going almost into a free fall as it moved to attack Alessande.

It was the perfect opportunity—exactly what he needed.

He went into a deadly dive and landed on top of the massive hawk. He bit hard and deep. The two of them began to tumble together, but he amped himself up in size and pulled up—fangs still buried deep in the shifter's flesh—just in time to keep them from slamming onto the cement of the parking area.

The falcon alit beside him, transforming back into Alessande in the blink of an eye.

Mark himself reverted to full vampire form, clasping the shapeshifter tightly before withdrawing his fangs. Alessande stepped closer, and together they looked at their attacker as it, too, reverted to human form.

"Brigitte," Alessande breathed. "Brigitte Hildegard."

Brigitte began spewing oaths at them as Mark held her to the ground. She clutched the back of her neck, where Mark's fangs had sunk into her.

"Have you got anything we can use as a bandage?" Mark asked Alessande. "She's bleeding to death."

Alessande ripped off the bottom of her shirt, then wrapped the admittedly filthy fabric around the downed shapeshifter's neck. By the time she finished, Brigitte was no longer speaking; she was unconscious.

"Let's get her back to Castle House," Alessande said, looking at him. "I can try to heal her there."

"She nearly killed us," Mark muttered, throwing the woman over his shoulder.

"She's all we've got," Alessande said.

She was right, of course. Brigitte might well be the connection they needed.

Or she might be the head of whatever was going on, though on reflection he doubted that. She was a follower by nature. Somebody else had to be pulling her strings.

Alessande sat in the backseat with Brigitte sprawled half on her lap as Mark drove. The box of ashes lay on the console between the two front seats.

He looked back now and then, making sure that Brigitte wasn't playing at being unconscious, even though he knew better. He'd taken a lot of blood.

He turned down Laurel Canyon Drive and then started the climb up to the House of the Rising Sun. He used the remote in the car to open the gate as he drew near.

In the yard, Wizard barked insanely. By the time he was parked, people were spilling out of their various houses—everyone in robes or pajamas.

"What the hell?" Brodie asked. "That's Brigitte Hildegard."

"Remember the corpse of the old woman? That was Brigitte," Mark explained dryly. "She had a remarkable transformation into a tiger and then into a hawk the size of Kansas."

They took Brigitte to Barrie's house because, as Keeper of the Laurel Canyon shapeshifters, she had the best provisions for the incarceration of a shape-shifter, and if they were able to heal Brigitte, she would be a danger anywhere else.

Rhiannon raced into Pandora's Box to find the medical equipment to give Brigitte a transfusion. She kept supplies on hand since she never knew when a vampire would come to her needing help.

Barrie's basement was soundproof and could be completely sealed—ensuring that no shapeshifter could become a worm or a roach and escape through a crack in a door or window. Brigitte was quickly laid out on a couch there and the process of the trans-fusion begun.

Alessande spent several minutes preparing a po-tent herbal tea, one with healing properties, so it would be ready to administer when—if—Brigitte regained consciousness. "Is she going to make it?" she asked anxiously on her return.

Rhiannon nodded. "She's getting some color back now. I think she'll come to soon."

As they waited, Mark glanced at his watch. It was morning; the mortuary staff would be there by now and wondering why one of the windows was broken—from the inside. He excused himself and made a call to Lieutenant Edwards, to bring him up-to-date on the night's events.

"Keep an eye on her—don't let her escape," Ed-wards ordered.

"She's safe. We've got her in Barrie's basement," Mark explained.

"All right. Now get those ashes dumped in the Pacific as soon as you possibly can."

"Yes, sir, will do," Mark promised and rang off.

When he returned, Alessande was seated near Brigitte, watching over her. He couldn't read her expression, but he was amazed once again that she always proved to be so much more than he expected. She had known just what to do to give him the chance to take Brigitte down.

"I think she's going to come out of it, but it may take a little time," Rhiannon said. "Barrie, you and Mick need to get to work at the paper. We don't want to draw suspicion by doing anything out of character."

"We need to scatter Sebastian's ashes right away," Mark said.

Declan stepped forward, "Sailor and I can handle that."

"Works for me," Sailor said. "I don't need to be at work until later. And it looks like my acting career is going to get lost in the disaster of yet another movie *not* being made." She smiled wryly. "It's okay. I *will* make it one day."

Declan pulled her into his arms. "Yes, you will. But for now, let's get moving. Rhiannon, we'll head straight back here when we're done."

"I wonder if one of us should stand guard outside," Alessande said.

Rhiannon smiled at her. "No need. We have Wizard and Jonquil."

The next thirty minutes seemed longer to Mark than the nearly three hours they'd spent at the mortuary. He and Brodie paced, passing each other in the small space every few seconds.

"Stop!" Rhiannon finally begged them.

Brodie nodded and sat down with his back against the wall. Mark perched at the foot of the couch where Brigitte lay.

Finally Rhiannon removed the IV apparatus. Brigitte had more color, but she still wasn't stirring.

"You haven't given up, have you?" Mark asked.

Rhiannon smiled, shaking her head. "She's gotten all she can take. She'll come around soon."

Five minutes later, Brigitte moved at last. Her head twisted, and she groaned. Then her eyes opened and she stared at them with loathing.

"You worthless bastards," she said, her voice whispery. "You don't deserve to be what you are. You are less than the weak humans who people this world like ants!"

"Right, whatever," Mark said, staring at her. "Now talk. Who is the head of the Cult of Tyr trying to raise your great-grandfather?"

She stared at him and blinked hard. Then she smiled. "Stupid. I'm the head of it."

"No, you're not," Alessande said. "You're a follower. It's not enough for you that you're living a great life—you want to be a queen, or a princess.

You want Sebastian back because you believe he'll give you the power you crave. But you're not the head of anything."

"Yes, I am. Why won't you accept that, Elven witch?"

"Because you're too foolish and ignorant to be the head of anything," Alessande said calmly. "And I'm so sorry, but you're not hurting my feelings at all. Some of my dearest friends are witches."

Brigitte swore at that and tried to turn away from them, but Brodie held her fast.

"You were at the tomb the night Brodie and I came in, weren't you? You escaped as a bug or a toad, I'll bet—very fitting, by the way," Mark said. "And you tried to kill Alessande and me the next night."

"I *will* kill you—eventually," she swore sweetly. "I mean, seriously, just what are you going to do now? Kill me and then tell my brother what you did? He wouldn't like that."

"I don't think he'd like what *you* did tonight, either, Brigitte," Brodie said. "I think Alan is very fond of his lifestyle. He doesn't want anyone getting in the way of that or taking power away from him—not even you."

"He won't let you hurt his sister," Brigitte insisted.

"We don't intend to hurt you. But we *will* make you talk," Alessande said, leaning closer to the prisoner. Mark had never seen her look more merciless and terrifying—not even as an avenging peregrine falcon. "We want to know where to find Regina Johnson."

But Brigitte seemed serene. "You are all so foolish. It's begun, and there's nothing you can do to stop it. It would have been nice if things had worked out at the tomb that night. But that wasn't the end. All your friends managed to do was delay us. Sebastian will return. You've failed."

"And you're a terrible liar," Alessande said.

That caused Brigitte to frown for a moment. But then she smiled again, slowly. "Do you really think that you could destroy Sebastian? He's more powerful than you can possibly imagine. You will all die—and I will be lifted up. I *will* be a queen," she told them.

"Where is Regina Johnson?" Alessande demanded again.

Brigitte was thoughtful. "I don't know."

"You *do* know," Alessande accused her.

"No, you can torture me from now to the Apocalypse, but it won't matter. I really don't know where Regina is right now," Brigitte said.

Alessande looked as if she was about to pounce. Brigitte shrank back into the couch, but before Alessande could address her lie and smack the woman, she stood and walked away.

Mark rose and went over to join her.

"I know what I said before, but can I torture her anyway?" she asked through clenched teeth.

"Alessande..."

"Yeah, yeah, that would make us as bad as she is."

"I'm not sure that's really my point right now, but I don't want to lose her. I have a better idea. We'll leave her with Rhiannon and Brodie, and go get Alan and Charlaine. Let them talk to her."

Alessande arched a brow. "That just might work— I guess."

Mark turned to Brodie. "I'm going to take Alessande out for a bit, see what we can dig up."

"You won't dig up anything," Brigitte said confidently. "I am the priestess. I am the head of the cult, and you will be sorry you ever crossed me."

"Take care," Rhiannon said. "And don't worry about our friend here—she doesn't have the strength of a two-year-old at the moment. And I can always rip out her throat if I choose to."

"No violence, hon," Brodie warned.

"I say cuff her, at least."

"I will turn into a crocodile and eat your heads," Brigitte promised.

Alessande laughed. That had probably been the greatest insult Brigitte could have received, with its implication that she couldn't even shift her way out of handcuffs.

Mark and Alessande left then, taking the Charger and heading toward the Hildegard mansion.

As they navigated the canyon, she looked through a grove of trees atop a cliff to a scene that seemed oddly familiar. "Mark!"

"What?"

"Stop. Please, stop."

He pulled off the road. She got out of the car and walked through the trees, feeling a chill settle over her as surely as if they'd been hit by a sudden ice storm.

"What is it?" Mark demanded, catching up to her.

"Look," she said, pointing. "The road to reach it must be just around on that bend we passed. Mark, it's—"

"The church from the wedding," he finished.

She swung around and stared at him, the chill deepening. "You saw the same church, didn't you? In your vision?"

He nodded.

She swallowed, noticing the strange look in his eyes. He wasn't afraid, but it was the look of a man facing the unknown.

"I'm going to investigate," he said. "You need to—"

"What? Are you crazy? I am *not* waiting in the car and we are *not* splitting up."

He smiled. "I wasn't going to suggest that. I was going to say that you have to be very careful. And I mean *very* careful."

She smiled. "Okay."

"Give me your hand. Let's walk up there. If we drove, our engine would warn anyone that we're coming."

She agreed with that. As they approached, however, she pulled him back. "Maybe one of us should shift," she suggested.

He looked at her dryly. "Well, I can do a large wolf or a bat. If there *is* a legitimate clergyman up there, I think either one would be extremely disturbing to him."

"Ferret?" she asked him. "I can curl around your neck and watch from there."

"I like the sound of that," he teased.

She started to tell him that he needed to be serious, but then she realized that he was joking for her sake.

"Should we call the others first?" she asked softly.

"We'll just take a look right now," he said. "Come on, oh talented Keeper-to-be."

She smiled, transformed and crawled up his body to settle around his neck.

Touching him in any way, she realized, felt good. And it made her feel secure to curl around his neck and absorb his heat as they moved up the hill.

The church was beautiful. It was small, but built in the Gothic style, like New England churches. It was whitewashed, with stained-glass windows. There was a graveyard next to the church and stretching around the back.

Mark paused and read the welcome sign aloud. "'St. Ann of the Little Flower, erected 1893,'" he said. "'Welcome all of Faith. Father Lars Gunderson, pastor.'"

Gunderson. Lars Gunderson. He was an Elven! She knew him from council meetings.

"It looks like a perfectly nice church and nothing more," he said. "I'm going in."

He walked up the brick path to the front steps. When he opened the door, he paused, letting his eyes adjust to the dimness, then looked into the interior.

Alessande could see that it was indeed the church she'd seen in her nightmare. The central aisle led to a large and richly decorated altar, with sacramental objects sitting on it. A golden cross took pride of place in the middle.

The windows allowed light to streak through, taking on the colors of the glass.

And a blood red runner ran down the aisle.

Mark started walking toward the altar.

"Maybe I was here when I was a kid," he said softly. "I do feel that I know this place."

"Hello, welcome to St. Ann's."

As Mark turned, Alessande saw that a man in priestly garb was walking toward them. She studied him quickly, then ducked beneath Mark's jacket, peering out but taking care to remain hidden.

"Welcome, welcome. I'm Father Lars Gunderson—Father Lars to my parishioners and friends, and I hope I can call you a friend," the priest said.

Mark offered him a hand. "A friend, yes. I'm Mark Valiente. I saw your church from the road. It was so beautiful, I had to investigate."

"Yes, she *is* pretty, isn't she?" Father Lars said.

"I'm lucky to be assigned here." He stopped, looking curiously at Mark. "You're staring rather strangely."

"Am I? Sorry. I'm just a bit in awe. I'm from this area, and I've never noticed the church before."

"We're up on the hill, hard to see from the road. We have a fine supply of parishioners, though. And we do our best to give back to the community."

Mark dug in his pocket and produced one of his cards. "Father, in all honesty, I'm a cop. And we've been having some trouble in the Valley, girls disappearing—"

"And dying," Father Lars said gravely. "I'm not barred from reading the papers, you know."

"Of course. I'm just curious. Have you had new parishioners lately? Or noticed anyone unusual hanging around or…had any break-ins, anything like that?"

"The rectory is down the hill, so I don't always see what's going on," Father Lars said. He hesitated. "But, yes—someone did break into one of the alms boxes about a week ago."

"Did you call the police, Father?"

The man smiled. He really *was* the perfect priest—warm smile and cheery red cheeks, deep brown eyes and salt-and-pepper brows. "Father" was a good fit; he would probably have been a great dad, gentle and patient.

"Detective Valiente," Father Lars said, "when a man is desperate enough to break into an alms box, I trust in God that he needed the money. No, I didn't report the theft. What could the police have done anyway?"

"Father, thank you for your time," Mark said. "I'm glad to have had the chance to see your beautiful church."

He was surprised when the priest smiled with a touch of bemusement. "I'm happy that my church can please a vampire. One living in the light, of course."

Mark was startled. "Father—"

"I am a friend to many Others," Father Lars said. "Please, come back anytime."

Mark shook the priest's hand again. Then he turned to leave and walked along the path. Alessande scurried around behind his back to watch as they moved away. She was sure that she saw dark shadows lurking by the side of the church, as if they were emanating from the graves. She felt a chill seeping into her again, despite the warm coat of fur she had given herself.

When they were back down the hill near the car, she scurried to the ground and resumed her true form.

"That's it," she said. "That's the church I saw in my nightmare. Well, the inside of it anyway. You were there, and Brodie and Rhiannon, and I was…"

"You were going to be killed," he said flatly.

"We have to use this knowledge, Mark. I believe we were given a warning. And I know Father Gunderson—I know him because he's Elven. Well, half Elven anyway."

He swore softly to himself. "Of course. I knew there was something about him."

She smiled. "It's because he's mixed. His father was Elven. His mother was human. I think he's spent most of his life being as human as he could. He's a good man, I know. I've seen him in the councils for years."

"We have to tell the others everything we saw in our dreams—maybe they'll know what it means," Mark told her. "For now, we need to go and get the Hildegards."

Mark knew that Alessande was suspicious of the entire Hildegard family—and with good cause.

After all, Brigitte had tried to kill them twice.

But both Alan and Charlaine looked so horrified and confused, Mark couldn't imagine that even shapeshifters could put up such a front.

Alan swallowed hard. "Is—is Brigitte all right? Forgive me—I understand that she tried to kill you, but…she *is* my sister."

"Brigitte is all right, but you have to understand that we're holding her and have no intention of letting her go," Mark said.

"But she's…safe?"

"Yes, she's safe. I gave her a good bite when she tried to rip me to shreds, but Alessande and the Gryffald cousins took care of her, and she's fine—conscious, and claiming to be the brains of the Bring Sebastian Back to Life movement."

Alessande spoke up then. "We need one of you to talk to her. We're getting desperate. Whoever is doing this is still keeping an Elven girl captive. We're trying to get her back before they use her in one of their rituals."

"Because if they do—she dies," Mark said.

"Let me get my jacket and we'll follow you in my car," Alan said.

As they drove back to the House of the Rising Sun, Alessande said, "The church is so close to the mansion and Father Gunderson said that he was a friend to the Other community. Do you think the Hildegards know that church? Maybe some of them have even attended services there over the years."

"It's quite possible," Mark said. "Likely, as a matter of fact."

The dogs greeted them enthusiastically on their arrival, then growled warningly as they saw Alan and Charlaine exit their own car.

"Are we all right?" Alan called.

"Unless you suddenly go crazy and attack one of us," Alessande said.

"We're here to help," Alan reminded her.

"Of course," Alessande said. "Please, follow me."

They headed for Gwydion's Cave, where Brodie let them in. Mark didn't give them time to admire the wonderful assortment of decorative artifacts as they passed through the house; he led them straight to the basement.

When Alan entered, they all stood back and let him take the lead. "Brigitte," he said sternly.

"Alan!" the youngest Hildegard gasped. For a moment she looked as if she were little more than a very innocent child.

Mark knew better. And glancing over at Alessande, he could tell that she was feeling the same.

"Brigitte, what have you done?" Alan asked, walking over to her.

Rhiannon, who had stayed to watch her, rose and backed away from the couch, allowing Alan room to sit down.

Brigitte seemed to shrink away from him slightly. "Alan, I... We are Hildegards! I read the diary years ago, and I knew that Sebastian was destined to come back. I only did what I had to do as a member of our family."

"Brigitte—you killed people!" he told her.

"No, I never killed anyone," she protested.

"Oh?" Alessande said angrily, walking up to stand at the foot of the couch. "Two women are dead, and you claim that you're the head of what's going on, so you killed them. They were held captive, held in terror—and then their throats were slit. Not to mention a junkie, a drug dealer and your own butler."

"Jimmy killed himself!" she cried.

"Out of fear of facing a more horrible death?" Mark suggested.

She swallowed hard. "Okay, I'm not the head of the cult."

"Then who is?" Mark hadn't meant to shout, but his voice was so deep and powerful that the room seemed to shake.

Brigitte definitely did.

"I don't know! A priest, but I don't know his name or even what he looks like," she swore. "I...I met him when I was bringing flowers to the tomb. He was wearing heavy robes, and he wore a gold mask under his cowl, and he told me that I was a Hildegard, so I had to help. I had to get the Transymil moving on the streets to make money, and I had to start showing up for the ceremonies, because Sebastian was waiting. And there was something about him.... It was as if I had no choice but to do what he said."

"So you were there when the other girls were killed," Rhiannon said harshly.

Tears suddenly welled up in Brigitte's eyes. "I was, but I didn't kill them!"

"Where were they killed?"

Brigitte hesitated, looking from each of them to the next. She was clearly about to deny that she knew, but then her brother lashed out at her.

"Where were they killed?" he demanded.

She exhaled and whispered. "At the church."

"At *what* church?" Alessande asked, her voice thick.

"The church by the house—St. Ann's."

There was silence in the room.

"I don't believe that!" Charlaine exploded. "I know Father Lars. He would never allow such a thing. He's a good man. And the church...the church has been consecrated!"

"They weren't killed *in* the church," Brigitte said. "There's a section of the cemetery, overgrown and filled with broken stones. It's where they've buried the dead-by-suicides since the beginning of the last century." She winced. "It isn't hallowed ground. Oh, my God, Alan, don't...don't be angry with me. Don't—don't turn away from me. I just wanted our family to rise to its full potential. I didn't want to kill anyone—really. I didn't. And when I saw that people were dying... I was afraid. I was afraid to back out. That's the truth—I swear it," she vowed.

Alan looked at Mark, seeking mercy for his sister.

"Barrie will be back soon. She's Keeper of the local shapeshifters. Brigitte's punishment will be a matter for her to decide," Mark said.

"I didn't kill anyone," Brigitte insisted again.

"You tried pretty damn hard to kill Mark and me," Alessande reminded her harshly.

"But...I failed. I probably failed because I didn't really *want* to kill you," Brigitte said.

"Why did you do it, then?"

Brigitte was sitting up, and she looked across the room at Mark. "I was ordered to kill you by the priest. He gave the orders for the girls to be taken. And he's the one who killed them."

"Why sell drugs? What was the money for?" Alessande asked.

"For the new world order, I suppose."

"Why didn't the priest approach your brother and you cousin?" Mark asked. "They're Hildegards, too."

"Because we aren't weak idiots," Charlaine said.

"Alan…" Brigitte begged, and grabbed his hands.

Alan disentangled himself and stood. "I'll ask our Keeper for mercy on your behalf, though I'm sure this will also be a council matter. People were killed," he said. "For now…"

"Take me home, Alan. Please, take me home."

He shook his head slowly, looking at her. "Brigitte, I can't. You were instrumental in multiple deaths, and you risked the very existence of the Other community. You will have to pay a price. Most of all, you have to take responsibility for what you've done. You should be grateful that you're alive right now. You might have died, too."

Brigitte didn't say anything, and Alan turned away from her and looked at Mark. "Will Charlaine and I be safe if we go home? I fear that whoever— and whatever—this priest is, he'll figure out that Brigitte has cracked. And what if he knows that we gave permission for you to dig up Sebastian and throw his ashes into the sea?" He turned back to Brigitte. "Did you tell him?"

"I—yes," she admitted.

Alessande walked over to her. "Where did you meet with him, Brigitte? And how often?"

"I don't know how often. Five times, maybe six. I went to the church—to the back. There's a huge oak. I perched there as a hawk, and when the priest came,

I transformed quickly and told him what I knew. I don't know how he knew I was there, but somehow he always did."

"And you've never seen his face?" Alessande demanded.

Brigitte shook her head. Tears were sliding from her eyes. "No. He always wore the gold mask, along with the cape and cowl. And each time I talked to him…"

"Go on," Alan said. "Each time you talked to him—what?"

"I was promised that we'd be royalty—Hildegard royalty—in the new order. That when Sebastian rose, he would rule the world."

Alan turned without a word and walked toward the door.

"Don't leave me!" Brigitte cried. "Please, Alan, don't turn away from me."

Alan looked at Mark, then back at his sister. "You'll be safe here, Brigitte. You've been lucky to be captured by Others, held by Keepers, not the human law. Thank your lucky stars that you survived—and that you just might have a chance at having a life again."

Ignoring her wailing, he walked out. Mark followed and caught up to him at the bottom of the stairs.

"What do I do now?" Alan asked. "I don't believe that Charlaine and I are safe."

Brodie joined them, firmly shutting the door to

the sealed room. "He's right, Mark. They *won't* be safe. They're going to have to hunker down here. They can sleep over at Pandora's Box. You and Alessande can stay at Castle House with Sailor and Declan, and Rhiannon and I will stay here, guarding our captive with Barrie and Mick."

Mark figured there was no reason not to speak plainly in front of Alan Hildegard. "What if this is all a ruse? We'll have our enemies right here in the compound."

"We have Wizard and Jonquil," Brodie said. "And other…forms of security."

Mark realized that Brodie was referring to Merlin, who could easily keep an eye on the Hildegards—and report anything suspicious.

"That's fine," Mark said. "But work or no work, we need everyone back here now. We know where to look for the priest who seems to be the head of the cult, so now we have to find him before he realizes we know more about what's going on."

"Mark."

He turned around and saw that Alessande was standing there.

"I know exactly what we should do to stop this—and stop this now."

"What?" he asked.

"Plan a wedding."

Chapter 13

Alessande was as surprised as anyone else by what she'd said—not to mention that she had meant it. Well, actually, she'd meant it as a sham, but when Mark had looked at her, she realized that in fact she had *really* meant it. And when he smiled, she knew that *he* meant it, too.

Mark started to laugh. She knew that Brodie and Alan were looking at the two of them as if they'd gone mad. And then, to her amazement, Mark suddenly fell to his knees and took her hand. "Alessande, I've never really had a chance to say this, and I'm not particularly good with flowery words—"

"You're a vampire," she told him, her lips twitching in a smile. "It's all in the eyes."

"True, but right now I think it's appropriate to

speak, as well. I love you. I want to spend the rest of my life with you. Will you do me the supreme honor of becoming my wife?"

There was nothing to do but join him down there on the floor and whisper yes as he kissed her hand.

"Are they crazy?" she heard Alan ask Brodie.

"Crazy in love, I guess," Brodie said.

"But…what does this have to do with…what we're facing?" Alan asked.

"I'm sure it's a long story," Brodie said.

"It is," Mark said. "And we'll tell it as soon as everyone's here."

"Just trust me when I say that this wedding might well be a catalyst in solving this case," Alessande added.

Later that night, with Declan standing watch over Brigitte and Merlin keeping an eye on Charlaine and Alan at Pandora's Box, the rest of the group gathered in the Castle House dining room, where Mark and Alessande explained about the dream and everything that they felt for each other.

In the middle of their conversation, Mark received a call from Bryce Edwards. He excused himself and went into the next room to talk. When he returned, he told them, "Well, our forensic accounting unit made some intriguing discoveries. Blue Dove Entertainment is—as we believed—legitimate. The owners are hardworking and honest. However, their last movie out—*The Devil Takes London*—"

"I saw it—it was wonderful," Sailor said.

"Have to admit—I loved it, too," Rhiannon said.

"We're digressing here," Brodie cut in. "What about the movie, Mark?"

"It was a critical hit, and the general consensus is that everyone involved will be up for all kinds of honors come awards season, but it was expensive to make and Blue Dove is still struggling to get out of the red. It's a situation that should be rectified once DVD sales, cable rights and all the rest are in, but in the meantime, the studio was very wary of making another investment that big."

"Okay, but isn't that why one of Alan Hildegard's companies-within-his-company got involved?" Alessande asked.

"Yes, but it turns out there's another company providing some of the financing, too. Gnome Entertainment," Mark said.

"Gnome Entertainment? So should we be talking to the gnomes?" Alessande asked.

"Too obvious, don't you think?" Rhiannon said.

"So what did the forensic accountants discover about this Gnome Entertainment?" Brodie asked.

"They're on it—they'll let us know as soon as they find out anything," Mark said. "Meantime, I'm going back to see Father Lars Gunderson in the morning. We need to hold this wedding as quickly as possible, and with St. Ann's involvement in our dreams as well as Brigitte's mystery priest—and I fervently hope Father Lars is not our man—it's crucial that we have the ceremony there."

"Mark, you just can't plan a wedding that quickly," Barrie said. "I mean, not if you want people to come. And if you expect to the get the church and the reception venue and—" She got a look of dawning understanding and broke off. "Mick and I will make sure that it gets into the paper as soon as you have Father Gunderson on board."

"In that case, I don't think we're going to have a problem with our guest list. I think they'll all arrive right on time," Mark said.

"You guys are crazy," Rhiannon said.

Alessande smiled at her. "We know."

That night, when they went upstairs to bed, Alessande threw herself into Mark's arms. "I love you," she said in a rush. "How is that possible? How did it happen so quickly? How can I be so sure that I never want to live without you again?"

"The same way I can," he assured her. "I just *know.*" He held her face tenderly between his hands and kissed her lips.

"You're ridiculously headstrong, you know," he told her a few minutes later, when he finally stopped to breathe.

"You like to take charge."

"You take chances."

"You move in like a bull in a china shop."

"But those eyes of yours…"

"Those eyes of yours…"

"The feel of your skin…"

They dissolved into a tangle of clothing, kissing and touching, and finally making love. It was late, very late, when Alessande lay incredibly content at his side, ready to sleep. It seemed ridiculous to be this happy when a young woman was still threatened with a cruel and bloody death. But she felt renewed hope that they were on the verge of solving this case at last and finding Regina Johnson safe and alive.

It was amazing to think that, in searching for Regina, she had found someone she needed as much as she needed air to breathe—and that she could and would wake up beside him every morning of her life to come.

But when she drifted to sleep, the dream of her wedding came again.

There was the church.

The church they had seen that very day.

And the music playing.

Music she loved and would have chosen....

She saw the white of her gown, and she saw the smiling faces of her friends.

And then she felt the shadows encroach as she walked down the red runner and it slowly became a sea of blood.

She woke up, shaking. She tried not to move, so as not to wake Mark.

But he was already awake. He was standing at the window, looking over at Pandora's Box.

"Mark?" she asked, rising and slipping over to stand by him.

"They seem so real, so honest, but are they?" he asked, and she knew he was referring to Alan Hildegard and his cousin Charlaine.

"Those tears Brigitte cried today seemed real," she told him as she wrapped her arms around his naked waist and laid her cheek against the breadth of his back.

"What are we missing?" he asked softly. "Because we *are* missing something, something we're not seeing."

"I don't know, but I think we will see it soon."

He turned, drawing her to face him, tilted her chin up and said, "This may be crazy, getting married so quickly, but...I think it's what we have to do. And, I swear, Alessande, I won't stop until we find Regina Johnson."

She rose on her tiptoes and kissed him. "I believe in you," she said, "with all my heart. I believe in you, and I love you."

He kissed her again. "We've got to get some sleep. Before I go see Father Gunderson, Brodie and I are going to tear apart the old Hildegard Studio again. See what we can find."

"Just for safety's sake, I'll get Sailor and Declan to go with me to the church, because I'd like to speak with Father Gunderson, too. I'll call him and tell him what we want to do, then you can meet us there."

"We should get an early start, so we really need to get to sleep."

But it was some time before they actually slept again. As Alessande drifted off, she realized that she hadn't said anything to Mark about having the dream again.

She hoped it wasn't a bad omen.

"This seems to get more and more confusing as we go along," Brodie said, sinking down into the couch where they'd found the screenplay for *Death in the Bowery*.

"I know. Is it really over money—or ritual murder?" Mark said.

Brodie shook his head. "Did they discover that the drug could render victims pliable and then that it could make big money on the street? Or vice versa?"

"I don't know. I *do* know that we've torn this place apart and there's no sign that anyone is being held here." Mark's phone dinged to indicate an incoming text, and he looked down at the screen. "They still haven't figured out who owns Gnome Entertainment. All they know so far is that it's headquartered in the Cayman Islands." He pocketed the phone. "Well, let's get over to the church. We have to set things up for the wedding."

"Crazy," Brodie said for the thousandth time. He glanced at his own phone as it beeped.

"Edwards?" Mark asked.

"No, Rhiannon. With good news."

"What's that?"

"Merlin reported that Alan admitted to Charlaine that he was afraid if someone did resurrect Sebastian, *he'd* be in for a torturous death. Makes him sound as innocent as he claimed to be."

"Here's hoping," Mark said. "Did she say anything about Brigitte?"

"Just that she's still safely locked in the basement."

"Good," Mark said, then paused as they started to head out. "Hang on, I want to recheck the soundstage with the cemetery scene."

"With the decaying corpses coming out of their graves?"

"Yep, that one."

"We already searched it."

"I know, but…something is sticking in the back of my head."

"What is it?" Brodie teased when they got there. "The zombies aren't scaring you, are they?"

"It's not the zombies at all," Mark said.

"Then what?"

"It's the headstones. The way they're set—I feel as if I've seen them before."

"Where?" Brodie asked.

"At the church. St. Ann's."

"A wedding gown is the first thing on the agenda," Alessande said. "I can't get married without a gown."

"That could take forever," Sailor said. "And we need to be going to the church."

"I know, but it won't take long, only about thirty minutes," Alessande assured them. She was seated at the table, whipping through websites on Barrie's computer.

"Aha! I found it," she said.

Barrie, Rhiannon and Sailor all rushed over.

"Gorgeous, very medieval, very…Elven," Sailor said.

"Are you sure that's the one you want?" Barrie asked her.

"Positive," Alessande said, looking up at them. "I've already seen myself wearing it."

Mark stood in the church graveyard, staring at the graves.

There were no zombies clawing their way out of the ground, but he had been right. The crooked old stones were arrayed just as they had been set up on the soundstage. Even the big old oak tree—with its branches dripping with Spanish moss, tired and mournful looking—matched the fabricated oak on the soundstage.

He was at the rear of the church, standing on the unconsecrated ground—the ground where the dead-by-suicides had been buried. Most of the stones were illegible now, the lettering worn away by wind and time, or obscured by mold and moss.

"You're definitely on to something here," Brodie said, walking up beside him.

"Since Sebastian was around at the time the filming was going on, I guess it was natural he told the designer to create a set that resembled something he knew. He probably sent him here to check it out, or gave him photos to work with." He looked speculatively up at the old tree. "And this is also where Brigitte said she met with the masked priest."

"There's definitely no one here now," Brodie said.

"No," Mark agreed. "But..."

"But?"

"I don't like it."

"Come on. The others will be here any minute. We have your wedding to set up."

In the few days until the wedding they split up their duties, watching over the Hildegards in Pandora's Box and the Hildegard being held captive in Barrie's basement.

They continued searching for clues in the disappearance of Regina Johnson but came up empty.

And yet Mark felt a ray of hope.

True, they hadn't been able to find her and free her.

But neither had they found her dead.

Friday evening they decided to have a rehearsal dinner at the Snake Pit.

They brought Charlaine and Alan Hildegard, and

Lieutenant Edwards gave up his evening to sit watch over Brigitte so all the Gryffald cousins and their fiancés could attend.

It was when Alessande was on her way back from the ladies' room that she ran into Greg Swayze.

"Hey, congratulations," he told her. "I was... stunned when I heard. I hadn't really realized you two were a couple. I mean, well, I wouldn't have asked you out if I'd known."

"No need to feel bad. We were on a break at the time."

"That wasn't that long ago."

"I know. But then..." She smiled encouragingly. "You're good-looking and talented. I'm sure you have no trouble meeting women."

"The thing is, I don't want a woman who—well, who wants to use me just to get a part," he said.

She grimaced at that. "Well, I did meet you because of the film."

"Yeah, but you're one strange actress. You practically told me that you didn't want the part."

She shrugged. "I'm not much of an actress. I do like extra work, though. I don't have to do anything but show up and then get paid."

He smiled and touched her hair. "Well, you're one of the good ones who got away. I always seem to be taken by tall blondes with blue eyes." He paused for a moment, looking thoughtful. "I met another actress who fit that description and was right for the part. She was enchanting. Regina, her name was."

"Regina Johnson?" Alessande asked.

"Yes," Greg said. "I can't believe you know her. I met her several months ago, right when I was trying to get the project going. I was infatuated. She read the play and said she loved it, so I had her read for me.

"I told her that the decision on whom to cast wasn't going to be mine and that there would be auditions, but I had hoped she'd do an official reading. But then...I lost touch with her."

Alessande stared at him. "She's missing, Greg. That's why you haven't heard from her. You know that Mark and Brodie are cops—they're looking for her, along with half the LAPD. If by any chance you *do* hear about her or from her, please let me know. We're desperate to find her."

"Missing," he said. Then his eyes widened. "Oh, no! Those two women who were murdered, they were actresses, too, and—oh, my God. They looked like her."

Alessande nodded.

"You have to find her!" he said.

"We will, Greg. We will," she promised.

She hurried back to the table, where Brodie was leading a silly toast to Mark. The minute he finished, she leaned in and told them what she had just learned.

Mark slipped an arm around her shoulders. "That confirms her connection to the film, which is great, but it doesn't get us any closer to finding her. But tomorrow—"

"We'll flush them out," she finished for him.

"And it will also be the best day of my life," he declared.

Chapter 14

Father Lars Gunderson appeared to be quite calm, a notable achievement, seeing as they had filled him in on the circumstances. The only thing that had upset him at the beginning was his impression that he would be staging a sham wedding.

But then Mark had assured him that he wouldn't be faking the wedding, which was going to be 100 percent real.

Real.

The thought made Mark tremble.

He knew beyond a doubt that he'd been waiting for Alessande all his life. That seeing someone as he saw her, needing someone as he needed her, being happy just to share a room—not to mention a bed— with her, was what he had waited all these years to know, to have. He loved her, plain and simple, and he wanted to marry her, to have children with her, to see what traits they might carry, what talents they might or might not have.

At the beginning, he realized, she *had* meant to stage a sham wedding, something to precipitate what they had seen in their visions. But the minute he had spoken, they'd both known it was real, that whatever the future held, they would face it together.

And now it was happening.

The Hildegard family—including Brigitte—would be in attendance. *Death in the Bowery* was well represented, too. Greg Swayze, Katrina Manville, Tilda Lyons, Milly Caulfield and Taylor Haywood had all been invited. As had Antony Brandt, Hugh Drummond and Jerry Oglethorpe, of the House of Illusion, not to mention Bryce Edwards and every Other on the police force.

Whatever danger showed, they should be covered.

It was a shame that their wedding had to be so rushed because a woman's life was at stake. But whatever happened, the marriage would be real.

The ceremony was planned for dusk. They would make their vows just as the sun began to fall in the western sky. Since a number of human beings would be among the guests, they'd decided jokingly that they weren't going to say anything about the hundreds of years they both hoped to live. But whether they lived ten or another ten hundred, it didn't matter.

Mark knew that he would love her forever.

The church began to fill up. The line of parked cars extended down the hill from the building to the street. Women arrived wearing spring colors that glowed in the gentle light of the waning sun.

Alessande would be here soon, along with the Gryffald cousins. Declan had provided the women with a white stretch limo for the day.

In one of the choral rooms, with Brodie standing by as best man, Mark took a long look in the mirror. The third tux he'd been shown had been the one he'd seen himself wearing in the vision. It was old-fashioned in style, charcoal-gray, worn with a white shirt and red vest.

"This is crazy," Brodie told him for the several-thousandth time. "You do realize you haven't even known each other a full two weeks."

"We have a long, long time ahead of us," Mark told him.

"We could have tried a different strategy. I mean, for all we know the cult won't even show up to this wedding. We'll end up no closer to the truth, and the two of you will still have rushed into a wedding."

But Mark shook his head. "I believe in certain truths. That the greatest 'religion' we can follow is that of being as decent as we can to our fellow man, standing up for those who need our help and doing the right thing when we can. As Others, we spent years segregating ourselves, and even now, no matter how well we live our lives, some will still disapprove, will refuse to accept a union between vampire and Elven, even though Alessande herself is already of mixed blood. But that's their loss. The point is, I know I love Alessande. I know that she loves me. And this wedding is what's supposed to happen for the two of us. As far as I'm concerned, our visions were just a warning that we have to be careful today—and you can't be much more careful than we're being here."

Brodie sighed. "I hope you're right about that. About all of it." He walked over to the door and opened it to look into the sanctuary. "It's filled up— wow. So much for no one coming on such short notice."

"Are the Hildegards here? Is Brigitte between Alan and Charlaine?"

"They're flanking her like a pair of gorgons," Brodie assured him. He shook his head. "We know that Brigitte was part of it. And we have the rest of the movie people here, as well. If any of them are in on it, too, we could be facing real trouble."

"And we're prepared," Mark assured him. He walked over to the door and looked out himself. He felt reassured by what he saw. Declan's massive leprechaun valet, Barney, was standing at the rear of the church. All those who could make it from his station house were there, including three werewolves, two shapeshifters, another Elven and four vampires. The cops—human and Other—were all armed.

As he stood there, Father Lars came to the door.

"It's time," he told Mark. "You need to take your places."

"The women are here?" Brodie asked, adjusting his collar.

"They are," Father Lars told him.

"I need to find Sailor," Brodie said, then looked at Mark and straightened his vest. "Good luck, buddy."

He left, and Mark followed Father Lars to take their places before the massive altar.

The organist began to play the theme from Zeffirelli's *Romeo and Juliet.* Declan and Rhiannon walked down the aisle together, since their significant others were best man and maid of honor. Barrie and Mick followed them and then next came Brodie and Sailor, who took their positions up front. Finally Hugh Drummond, the Keeper of the Laurel Canyon werewolves, appeared with Alessande on his arm.

She took Mark's breath away.

She looked like an angel, her hair a shimmering gold so pale it glowed like a crown beneath her veil. Her gown highlighted her figure and fell in classic folds. She moved with such grace that she almost appeared to be floating.

Everyone stood as she walked down the aisle. Mark had a feeling that if evil *was* there in the room with them, it was as smitten with the bride as everyone else appeared to be.

"Who giveth this woman?" Father Lars said, beginning the ceremony.

Hugh responded, then lifted Alessande's veil

and kissed her on the cheek. And, at last, she was standing next to Mark. For a moment, as their eyes touched, all danger and dark shadows were gone. *This is real,* he thought. *This moment is the most real of my entire life.*

As the ceremony continued, Mark wasn't even sure that he heard the words. But as Father Lars spoke, he felt that he was in a bubble of crystalline beauty. When they were pronounced husband and wife, he kissed the bride, humbled and trembling. He realized he had been kissing his bride just a little too long when he heard Father Lars clear his throat.

Everything had gone off without a hitch. And he was a married man.

They looked at one another and took a minute just to smile. But he knew that Alessande's smile was as careful as his.

This wasn't over yet.

They walked down the aisle, pausing to shake a hand here and there, or receive hugs and kisses on the cheek. When they stepped out of the church, their guests pouring out behind them, not only were they pelted with rice but Jerry, a magician from way back who owned the House of Illusion, had arranged for a flight of doves to soar into the heavens in their wake.

A second white stretch limo waited to take them to the House of the Rising Sun, where the reception was to take place. But as they greeted friends and the photographer ran around, trying to gather them all up for pictures, Mark felt a sense that something had changed.

He looked toward the western sky.

The sun hadn't quite fallen beneath the horizon yet. It was a low-lying fireball, sending streaks of orange and gold against the mountains and hills behind the church.

And as he watched, the church seemed to grow dark against that splendid explosion of color.

He realized that shadows were creeping around the church. Something dark had arisen, and it was coming toward them with slow menace.

"Alessande!"

She'd been lost in such euphoria that she'd nearly forgotten the danger of the dream—that they'd *seen* this day and it had been filled with darkness and blood.

But as Mark called her name in warning, she immediately remembered.

The danger promised by her dream had never been destined to arrive *in* the church. The church was consecrated.

As she turned, she realized that the wind had picked up with a sudden ferocity, as if a dust storm had risen from the graveyard. It burst over them with such force that she immediately heard screaming and shouting as people ran about madly trying to reach their cars and escape the whirlwind.

White and stricken, Charlaine Hildegard went

rushing by. Alessande caught her arm. "Charlaine, where's Brigitte?"

Charlaine looked like a woman in shock. She stared blankly at Alessande.

"Charlaine! Where is she?"

The woman blinked in fear. "The wind... The wind carried her away. I have to go. I have to *go*. Don't you see? He's back. Sebastian is back! Oh, my God, when he finds me... And Alan. I've lost Alan."

"Charlaine, get into the church!" Alessande said.

But it was no good; the woman was in a panic and raced away toward the parked cars.

A hand gripped hers. "Alessande, get into the church!" It was Mark, and she drank in his handsome face, his burning golden eyes, and felt his love, his concern—and his determination. "Go, please. You'll be safe in there."

"I have to fight, too."

"Not now, because it's you they're after. Please!"

He drew her to him, kissed her lips passionately but briefly. "Please, go. For me."

She winced and knew that he was right; this was one time when she would be a distraction and a danger rather than an asset.

But she couldn't reach the church.

So many people were running toward her that she was nearly trampled. She lost sight of Mark in the inky darkness surrounding them, swirling as if a twister had suddenly sprung to life. Despite her strength, she felt herself being carried by the wall of people running toward the parking lot.

Finally she fought free and forced her way through the crowd toward the steps. She could hear Mark shouting to everyone to get into the church, but no one was listening.

At last she reached the door. But when she tried to open it, she realized that it had been bolted shut.

Someone had slid the massive bolt that locked the front door.

She pressed herself against the building and tried to make her way around to the side door, but she knew in her heart that every entrance had been bolted just as the front door had been.

So be it.

She was forced away from the building by the crowd, and once again she was nearly trampled. People were screaming and shouting in raw panic.

"Zombies!" someone cried.

Zombies? It wasn't that they didn't exist—but they weren't the same as werewolves, Elven, vampires, shifters, gnomes and the rest of the Other races. They were reanimated; they had no minds. They were the dead brought back by magicians and illusionists, or those poisoned into a kind of limbo by voodoo priests and priestesses. They had no real life. They lumbered through the world with only one goal: to eat the flesh and drink the blood of the living.

They had to be stopped, and the vicious puppeteer pulling their strings had to be stopped, as well.

Someone fell in front of her; she bent down, helping the woman to rise. It was one of the hostesses from the Snake Pit.

"Help me!" she screamed.

Alessande took her by the arm and led her through the crowd, guiding the woman into her car.

She was suddenly buffeted against another vehicle. The door was open, and someone was rummaging inside. "Hugh!" she cried, recognizing the werewolf Keeper.

"Here!" He tossed something to her. She caught it quickly, without thinking, and realized it was a sword.

"Cut the heads off," he told her. "Nothing—no creature out there—can live without a head."

Before she knew it, he'd turned and was racing into the darkness. Half the cars were headed downhill but, judging by the crashing sounds she heard, they were plowing into each other rather than actually escaping.

Alone, she tossed away the remnants of her veil and fought against the wind to reach the rear of the church. As she came around the corner of the building, she paused, amazed by the sight before her, just visible in the darkness and swirling dust.

It was as if she had stumbled onto the set of a horror movie. Whoever was pulling these strings had raised every person who had committed suicide since the church had been built—and whatever other dead creatures had stumbled into the graveyard. She saw

Declan standing on a tombstone, wielding a gun. As she watched, he tossed the gun aside and morphed from a man into a tiger, and ripped out the throat of the nearest walking corpse, then kept ripping until the head was torn from the body.

Brodie was walking into the fray, using his Elven strength to rip them to pieces. She saw that Mick and Barrie were fighting back-to-back. Rhiannon had become a wolf and, like Declan, was tearing the undead apart with her teeth. Hugh walked past her, swinging a sword identical to the one he'd given her.

"Alessande! Oh, my God, Alessande!"

She felt trembling fingers on her arm and turned to see the costume designer, Katrina Manville, huddling behind her, her eyes wide-open with terror. "I don't believe it, I don't believe it," she repeated through chattering teeth. "It can't be real."

A corpse lunged at Katrina, who screamed in terror.

Alessande shot out a fist, knocking the thing down but not rendering it harmless. "Come on— I'll get you to a car," she told Katrina, then dragged her to the relative safety of the recessed side door.

"Can they get into the church? Are they zombies? Oh, God, this can't be real." Katrina practically sobbed.

"We can't get into the church—the doors are locked," Alessande said.

But Katrina ignored her and clawed at the door. To Alessande's astonishment, it opened.

"Get inside—quickly," Alessande commanded.

The terrified woman was still clinging to her, so she stepped in as well, trying to gently escape Katrina's hold. But even as she freed herself, she saw a length of fabric—a crimson cowl—flying at her. She lifted her arms to ward it off just as Katrina swung around and slammed her in the ribs with all her might.

The robe fell over Alessande's head, and she inhaled a sickly sweet scent as it draped itself over her face like something living.

Transymil.

She held her breath and fell to the floor, pretending that the drug had worked but staging her fall so that the cowl didn't completely cover her face, giving her a few sweet breaths of clean air.

Then she waited.

They'd brought guns loaded with silver bullets. Mark had never figured that they were going to need swords.

He cursed his lack of foresight but was glad to see that Hugh Drummond had been smart and carried an entire arsenal—swords included—in his car.

Mark was forced to transform, becoming a wolf and tearing into the lumbering dead intent on killing everything living. One after another, they came after him, but he didn't fight alone. Barney had settled in the old oak tree to rip off the zombies' heads as they passed beneath him. He saw his fellow policemen—including Lieutenant Edwards—fighting all-out against the monsters. As he watched, Edwards became a different sort of wolf, bigger, fiercer, able to stand on his hind legs and use his huge forepaws like hands, dealing death to the dead.

As Mark ripped another throat from one of the zombies he thought, *We will win this. There are enough of us, and we are stronger, smarter and better equipped to tear things to shreds.*

Then it struck him: they were meant to win.

But they were meant to fight a long battle.

And suddenly he knew why.

"Brodie!" he called.

Brodie looked his way.

"The church!" Mark roared, and ran for the building.

Alessande lay on the altar, pretending to be drugged but in actuality able to open her eyes just a slit and see what was going on.

She wasn't sure how—maybe the blood sacrifices of their human victims had given them the power?—but somehow the evil beings were now able to function inside a consecrated church.

The front door was now open and someone was standing there, just at the entry. He wore a golden mask, a cape and a cowl and cradled a dead man in his arms. Brigitte's evil priest, she realized, but who was he carrying?

Could that be the real corpse of Sebastian Hilde-

gard? Was that what Brigitte had meant when she'd said they couldn't destroy Sebastian? That they'd had the wrong body all along?

Three women were circling the altar and chanting.

The first was Katrina Manville.

Human.

Next came another human: Tilda Lyons, associate producer for *Death in the Bowery.*

The third was the shapeshifter Brigitte Hildegard.

Suddenly Tilda stopped chanting and said, "We've got to do it now—*now,* before someone gets in!"

"Finish the chant!" the priest in the doorway roared. "It won't work if you don't finish the chant."

Alessande was just able to see that Father Lars lay facedown in the long red carpeted aisle between the pews. She prayed that he was alive. She strained to get a better look at the figure at the end of the aisle.

The women stopped moving—and speaking. Alessande knew that at any moment a knife would plunge toward her, but still she tried to figure out who was wearing the mask and cloak.

"Now, Brigitte, now!" the priest commanded.

Brigitte turned. Alessande opened her eyes and stared up at her. Brigitte looked as pale as a ghost, holding a lethal-looking dagger tightly in her white-knuckled hands.

"Now!" the priest shouted again.

"I can't!" Brigitte cried.

The priest let out a terrible scream of fury. "You will pay for your insubordination!"

"No!" Brigitte cried, crumpling to her knees.

In a fury, the priest started moving. As he left the doorway and entered the church, fire kindled in the air and licked at his robes. Entering the consecrated ground of the church, Alessande realized, could prove fatal to him. He moved quickly, as if to stay ahead of the flames, skirting the prone body of Father Lars as he rushed to the front of the church.

He laid the corpse at the foot of the altar, then wrenched the dagger from Brigitte's lax hands.

The moment of truth was at hand.

As he raised the dagger, Alessande jerked up, knocking his arm aside and wrenching the mask away.

She gasped in shock. "Regina!"

"Damn it! Why can't you just shut up and die?" Regina Johnson screamed at her. She still held the dagger, and Alessande was frozen in complete surprise.

The dagger started its downward thrust....

Just as the door to the church swung open.

And there he was, filling the doorway, gun in hand.

Mark.

Alessande teleported.

Regina Johnson—not a victim but a killer—slashed fruitlessly with her dagger.

But it fell from her hands as Mark's bullet ripped straight through her heart.

For a moment there was silence.

Alessande reappeared at Mark's side. He felt her there, turned and took her into his arms.

It really was a mess.

Thankfully, there were lots of Other cops on hand, and Barrie and Mick were the first among the media.

As soon as they had assured themselves that Father Lars had suffered only a minor head injury and had him on the way to the hospital—Hugh Drummond driving—they began the cleanup.

And the cover-up.

A sudden storm had started things. And then the guests had imagined they were seeing zombies when a freak localized earthquake had forced the dead from their graves.

Mark would have to be debriefed. After all, he had fired a fatal shot, but they all knew he wouldn't have a problem claiming it a righteous kill, given that Regina had been about to skewer Alessande.

Katrina and Tilda had been arrested for conspiracy to commit murder, and no amount of babbling about the Cult of Tyr and zombies would change their fate.

Brigitte, a virtual puddle of tears, tried to explain things in her desperate attempt not to be handed into police custody. She reminded them over and over again that she hadn't been able to kill Alessande when it had come down to it. Whatever happened, Alessande thought, that one point did hit home with her.

Brigitte told them how she'd discovered that Sebastian Hildegard had never really been buried in his tomb. He'd murdered another elderly cancer patient with an overdose of painkillers and had him buried in his place. Then Sebastian had ordered his servants to bury him secretly in the unconsecrated graveyard in the back of the church. Brigitte had known that, but when she'd met Regina Johnson and had begun to conspire with her, she hadn't realized what evil her family tales would incite.

Or so she claimed.

While the cleanup and the cover-up were still going on, Alan and Charlaine returned. They joined Alessande, Mark and the others at the altar, looking down at the corpse that still lay sprawled there.

"Do you think he really could have been brought back?" Mark asked.

"I don't know, but I don't think we should take any chances," Charlaine said.

"Well, Hugh lent me something before he headed out." Mark reached down to the floor for Hugh's sword, and slashed off the dry and decaying head with an easy swing.

"Cremation, too," Alan said.

Lieutenant Edwards, who walked up in time to hear Alan's words, assured them, "I'll take care of that."

Charlaine set a hand on Alessande's arm. "What now? What about Brigitte?"

"They won't take her to prison—Lieutenant Edwards knows she'll just escape. Her fate will be left up to Barrie and a council of shapeshifters and shapeshifter Keepers," Alessande told her.

"May we take her home for tonight?" Alan asked. "I swear, we'll make sure she doesn't escape."

Mark looked at Alessande. She shrugged. "She did refuse to kill me. I think we can release her to her family for the time being."

It was nearly midnight when they were finally able to return to the House of the Rising Sun.

"Well, the reception was a bust," Alessande said, her hand in Mark's as she surveyed the stacks of food the caterers had left for them.

But Mark only smiled. "That's okay. We have the rest of our lives."

Epilogue

It was three months before the next wedding took place.

Alessande and Mark had enjoyed a fantastic honeymoon at a ski chalet in Switzerland.

While things had been a bit rough at first, *Death in the Bowery* had finally gone into production. Of course, a new costume designer and associate producer had to be found, but this was Hollywood, and when things needed to happen, they happened quickly.

Sailor was ecstatic to have won the leading role. Alessande was happy to play a victim, knowing she would never let herself be one in real life again.

So it was early fall when the wedding took place.

Alessande enjoyed every second of the preparations. She festooned the entire compound with leaves and seasonal decorations. She painstakingly created a large vine-covered arch for an altar, entwining the greenery with all manner of herbs that promoted health and wellness and the happiness she believed would come. Mark watched her work with amusement in his eyes and a smile on his lips.

The day came, and Father Lars, who'd become a good friend, arrived to officiate.

Once again the guest list included Others of all kinds, and human beings, too, of course.

When the time came, Alessande was the first to walk down the flower-strewn aisle, tossing rose petals as she went and holding tightly to her husband's arm.

Merlin—unseen by many, but known by the one who mattered most—walked Rhiannon down the aisle to give her over to Brodie. Hugh Drummond passed a stunning Sailor over to Declan, and Barrie was escorted by Bryce Edwards.

Father Lars read beautifully, and all three couples exchanged vows they had written themselves before being pronounced husband and wife, and husband and wife, and husband and wife.

Arm in arm, Alessande and Mark watched as their dearest friends were joined together. And this time the reception went off without a hitch.

And then they went home to sleep in Alessande's bed, her beautiful wooden bed where she gained her strength.